TECH TEENS

THE BEGINNING OF A SAGA

ADRIANA ROY

INDIA • SINGAPORE • MALAYSIA

ISBN 979-8-89186-589-1

Contents

Chapter 1 – Lost and Found

The Fading of Nathaniel's Flower was Devastating, yet he Stood Up. The Future Awaited – Filled with Twists and Turns.

13TH JULY

The sun was battling the dark clouds to reveal its presence, but the clouds, made of steel, had other plans. It was going to be a challenge for the sun to break its walls.

***

It was an ordinary day, like any other. Mariah was busy in the kitchen as usual while her younger son Nathaniel studied at the dining table while the elder son Raymond, reading a magazine. A phone call broke the routine. It was Ria, Mariah's daughter on the other end.

"Mum, are my lovely brothers at home now? How about we all had dinner together today? It seems like it has been decades since we all sat down and had a hearty meal together. I am missing so much the lovely conversations we used to have at the dinner table. By the way can you make a hot bowel of ramen for me? I am just few miles away and should be home soon unless the crazy traffic slows me down."

"Honey, take care and drive slowly as it is raining heavily. See you soon," Mariah sighed as she pressed the end button on her phone.

Who was that mum? Was that Ria? "What did sis say, mum? When is she coming back home?" Nathaniel asked as he continued doing his homework. He was Ria's elder brother and loved her dearly.

"Yes, that was your sister. She was asking about you and Raymond. She is on her way home and would like for all of us to have dinner together. Even though she sounded cheerful, I don't have a good feeling. I feel a heaviness in my chest." Mariah was never wrong about her instincts. This family was gifted with abilities which would unravel slowly.

"Don't worry mum, sis would be alright. She would be home soon enough", Said Raymond

Sadly, little did they realize that this was the last time they were going to hear from Ria.

***

It was 7:30 pm and still no sign of Ria. Almost half an hour had passed since Mariah had spoken to her daughter over the phone. Mariah started to worry now. That's when Mariah's ringtone rang again, "Ria is calling!"

"Why is Ria calling me again? Is she in some sort of trouble?"

Mariah's hands trembled as she tapped on the accept button. Her heart was racing. As they say, a mother knows.

"Hello, is this Mrs Mariah Walker," a stranger asked.

"Yes, this is she...... but, how do you know me? Who are you? And why are you calling from my daughter's number?"

"I am Jonathan, Mrs Walker. I am calling you from your daughter's phone. I am sorry to inform you, but she has met with an accident, and is in the operation theater. You have to come here quick."

Mariah went numb.

"WHAT.... ahh...which hospital..." Her voice trailed off.

"Boys, we need to go to the hospital right now. Our precious Ria has been critically injured in a car accident. She is in the operation theater."

The drive to the hospital was filled with tears and sobs. Raymond drove like a maniac leaving behind many horns as he raced towards the hospital without bothering about the speed limit.

***

At the reception, a young male receptionist was typing away on the computer. His name tag read Jonathan. He did not notice Raymond who was staring at him with bloodshot eyes.

"Jonathan, I am Raymond Walker, Ria's eldest brother. How is my sister?"

Jonathon looked away from his monitor and looked up at Raymond. He looked back at his screen and typed.

"Well, she had lost a lot of blood. She is fighting for her life. Please head down the corridor and at the end, is the emergency department. Someone will be able to provide you with a more accurate update," Jonathan pointed toward the corridor.

As Raymond turned around, he noticed that his mother had collapsed due to shock and his brother, Nathaniel was trying to get her back on to her feet. Raymond swiftly helped his brother to get their Mom to regain her posture back. The three of them then rushed towards the emergency department.

When they reached the emergency department, Raymond spotted a doctor standing at the hallway going through a chart. Raymond walked up to him and inquired about his sister.

"I am Dr Mark. I am the surgeon who operated on your daughter."

He looked at Mariah with a remorse in his eyes. He then lifted her hands and placed them over his as if ready to break some heartbreaking news.

"We tried our best to save your daughter. She had lost a lot of blood by the time she got here."

There was complete silence which lasted just about five seconds before Nathaniel let out a bloodcurdling scream. It tore across the room. It was followed by a scream from Mariah. This would haunt Raymond for months to come.

***

Three months later….

Nathaniel was crying silently as he looked at the rusty old frame which was on his bedside table. He lifted it and looked at the photo. That was taken when he was seven and Ria stood beside him with a bright smile. They had visited Disneyland that year and this photo was taken at the entrance. Nathaniel recalled what a fabulous family holiday it had been.

"Why? Why god? Why did you take away that special flower away from Raymond and me? That flower bloomed in every season, under every condition. Why? I cannot help but blame myself for her death. That accident has ruined our family forever. Ria Walker will never return!"

"Brother, I know it is hard for us to accept such a bitter reality, but if we keep looking back at our past, then, we will not be able to live our present. I am sure Ria would have wanted us to move on and live," Raymond hugged Nathaniel tightly.

"I feel that it was just yesterday that we lost her. I feel the loss and the pain. As her elder brother, I have seen her grow up to be that caring and loving daughter and sister the family was so proud of," Raymond continued.

"I know that Ria would want us to be happy, but we must find out that who took our sister away from us?

I feel a churning in my body. I feel there is some sort of electrical current raging inside me. Something is going to happen soon. I sense it," Nathaniel said.

"Nath, maybe that is what will help us seek revenge from the person who took away our sister and a daughter away from her mother?" As Raymond uttered these words, his eyes brimmed with tears.

Raymond and Nathaniel had always been close, but the death of Ria had brought them much closer. They had become inseparable and looked out for each other. They were determined to get to the bottom of Ria's death. They needed closure. They had to find out how Ria's car crashed just a few miles away from their home.

Nathaniel gently placed the frame back on the table and looked at Raymond. He knew as a team they would get justice for Ria.

***

The night passed the morning sun came which gave a sign for the brothers to head to school. Raymond took his car from the garage and called out to Nathenial who was waiting for him. The drive from home to school was just about 10 minutes. Raymond parked his car in the students parking lot, while Nathenial waited for his brother near the school door. Then when Raymond came both the brothers entered inside a huge corridor filled with big lockers and many students. As soon as the brothers entered inside, they heard a familiar male voice and they turned their necks on the right and saw…

"Good morning Nathaniel. I hope you are fine?" Pearce walked up to Nathaniel and placed his arm on his shoulder.

Pearce was a dumb but caring teenage boy. He had surprisingly good imagination and was exceptionally talented when it came to solving scientific problems. He was a good friend of the walker brothers as well as their sister Ria.

"I am great. Do I look ill to you?", replied Nathaniel.

"No, it's just that Raymond messaged us yesterday about the awkward feelings and sensations you have been experiencing. So, Kamran and I were just concerned for you and your health. It has been three months since Ria passed away…."

"I know, but I am completely fine, and I have given my word to Raymond that I will not look back at the past as it serves us no purpose and adds more grief.

Pearce looked at Nathaniel in the eye and said, "I get that, but what are you experiencing, exactly?"

Before Nathaniel could respond, Kamran yelled out, "Guys, it is time for our class. Let's head towards the classroom before Ms. Angela buries us alive."

"Nathaniel, if you don't mind, can I say something?" Kamran shuffled his feet.

"Yeah, go ahead."

"I… I think Ms. Angela may be rather happy that Ria is no longer alive. We all know how much she hated

Ria and made it so miserable for her in the class." Kamran said. He realized he might have spoken too much.

Nathaniel sighed.

"I swear, I hate her for that same reason. I mean, why and what was wrong with my sister that she hated her so much?"

In his heart, Kamran knew that Ms. Angela, who also happened to be his mum, cared deeply for Ria. She just had a bizarre way of showing it.

"I may have touched a raw nerve, but sorry Nathaniel, I did not say those things to offend you, but the day you learn about my dark history…I don't think our friendship will survive," thought Kamran to himself.

"Dear brother, I know you are showing only one side of yourself to everyone. I know how much you are hurting inside. I wish I could do something to cheer you up, but maybe this is a trial by fire we both have to go through," thought Raymond as he fiddled with his backpack strap.

Despite the sometimes harsh words, both brothers had to hear, and the looks of pity, both brothers showed a brave united front.

***

The friends headed towards their classroom and when they opened the classroom door all their classmates turned their necks towards the Walker brothers.

"Guys, stay strong. Everyone is looking at you pitifully. I have a feeling that this will not last for long," Pearce whispered.

"Arghh! This is so frustrating. The atmosphere is too dark for my liking. I am feeling this wave of negative energy flowing," Kamran chipped in.

"I hate to admit it, but I am feeling the same," Nathaniel added.

Raymond quietly contemplated, *"I have a feeling this is not going to go away that quickly. We still have Ms. Angela to deal with."*

***

As the boys entered the classroom, a hush fell over. A few students at the back were pointing towards Raymond and Nathaniel. The silence was short-lived.

"Nathaniel, Raymond, I am so sorry for your loss, guys. I know how hard these times are for you guys. We are all here for you," Daniel said. He walked up to both brothers and draped his arms over their shoulders.

"Thank you all. We feel very blessed and touched by the phone calls, messages, flowers, and home visits the last few months. Yes, it has been challenging time in our lives. But with your love and support, we will pull through," Raymond said quietly as he scanned the classroom. He noticed there was genuine care and concern in the eyes of the students.

Nathaniel, on the other hand, was beginning to have a heavy feeling in his chest. His head was hurting, and he was forced to keep his eyes open. He quickly sat down on his seat before it became evident that something was not quite right with him.

Just as Nathaniel sat, Ms. Angela entered the classroom. There was complete silence. Immediately, she gazed towards Raymond and Nathaniel. Her look alone was a dead giveaway.

"I am so sorry for your loss, boys. Ria was such an asset in the classroom. She was a delight to teach...oh she was so bright…."

Nathaniel and Raymond had both stopped listening a long time ago. When she first gazed at them, that slight smirk was detected by both brothers. It was game over for them. Ms. Angela was a hypocrite.

As the lesson continued, Nathaniel was bothered that his eyes were forcing a shutdown. He was trying hard for them not to close. This had been happening a lot recently. If only Ria had been here, she would have figured out something. At the thought of Ria, Nathaniel was brought down the memory lane as he recalled how Ria would run towards the cherry blossom trees and glance at them with her shining eyes.

Raymond had been observing Nathaniel, and he whispered, "Dude, I know your eyes are feeling that they are about to shut, but don't worry after class, just go and wash them."

Nathaniel nodded.

But there was something else in store. Even before the bell rang, Nathaniel's eyeballs suddenly turned blue. The next thing, the tube light right above him, burst. There was a loud pop, and a large glass piece fell to the ground, inches form his feet as electricity sizzled above.

Nathaniel was horrified. What just happened?

Raymond immediately stood up and asked his classmates to move to the back of the class. What was meant to be the job of Ms. Angela was overtaken by Raymond. Ms. Angela was nowhere to be seen. She had run out of the classroom! Nathaniel remembered Ria. She would have done the same, been there to protect her classmates.

"Guys, it seems to be an odd incident, out of the blue. Guys, I don't think we are in danger. Let's focus…" Raymond did not finish his sentence as the bell rang, and the students hurriedly picked up their bags and started shuffling out of the classroom.

Nathaniel smiled. Raymond ticked all the boxes to be class president.

The boys headed to the cafeteria in silence.

***

As Nathaniel played with his salad with the fork, he said, "Guys, I broke that light. It was me. I felt a spark in my eyes. The next thing I knew, I was staring at the tube light."

Kamran, Pearce, and Raymond stared at Nathaniel in disbelief. It took a few seconds to register what Nathaniel had just revealed.

"Prove it," Said Raymond with a cold look in his eyes.

Nathaniel pulled his chair back and got up. He walked over to the vending machine. He placed his hands in his pocket and stared at the food items. The boys back at the table thought that Nathaniel had lost it.

Suddenly, the machine whirred, and they heard a pop. Nathaniel casually bent over and picked up his favorite chocolate bar from the slot. He unwrapped the packaging and took a big bite as he walked over the table. The look on the boy's faces was priceless.

"The truth is, I have had this power for a while now. While it is useful, I don't know what it is called. I don't even know how I got it."

"To be honest, I think I know. Two days ago, I read a book in the library about such powers. The author was…", Kamran said as he scratched his head.

"Who was it?" Nathaniel interrupted him mid-sentence.

"The book was written by Adrian Lightwood. That guy was an inventor and a scientist, but he disappeared ten years ago, and it was an irreparable loss to the scientific world," Kamran continued.

"Guys, let's finish up lunch. I assume the book should still be in the library. That is where the answer lies," Raymond said with a curious tone in his voice.

***

It took a while for the boys to find the book in the library. Well, you know how it is. You will find all the books, but the one you look for, oh well, takes a while.

"Is this it?" Nathaniel pointed to an old book covered in dust and torn pages sticking out of it, lying on top shelf of a rack. (maybe a picture of this)

"Bingo! Yup, that's the one, "THE TECHNOPATHIC WALKERS."

"Not fair! Not fair at all! How is this even possible. The book's name is "THE TECHNOPATHIC WALKERS," and yet, I am a Walker, and I do not have the special powers!" Raymond scowled.

"This is called destiny. The owner does not choose the power; the power chooses its owner…" A voice whispered.

This voice had whispered in everyone's ear. They all stood paralyzed with fear. That sound was too familiar. Wait…wait…

"Guys, heard that? That whispering voice was so familiar; I felt as if I had heard that voice before…" Nathaniel could not complete his sentence.

"Yeah, this might sound funny to all of us but are you thinking the same thing that I am thinking? Raymond looked around.

"Do you mean?" Kamran could not talk further.

"The voice belongs to none other than Ria," Pearce said this very quietly.

Nathaniel broke into a smile, "Yes, that voice belongs to Ria."

"Guys, look over there, on the wall," Nathaniel pointed across the shelf. In a crazed excitement, everyone turned towards the wall. There was a tiny sticky tape and on it was a barely legible message which read: Grab your cycles and meet me where the Forbidden Ferry awaits you.

The boys were very excited. The mystery was deepening. First, Nathaniel's powers had come to light, and now someone had written a cryptic note. They stormed out of the library and made their way to the Forbidden Ferry. It was a dreadful and dreary place for meeting someone, yet they were excited as they hoped to find some clues leading to Ria's death.

As the boys left, the sticky tape mysteriously fell to the ground and surprisingly the words had just vanished and the note appeared to be completely blank. It was quite eerie as if the message was delivered to its rightful recipient and so it had to disappear too.

***

"Just look at this dreadful place. On the outskirts of town, this empty wasteland. It smells of death. This place has become an illegal dumping ground. Oh, the horrible smell," Nathaniel pinched his nose.

The Forbidden Ferry was a ship that had been illegally dumped on this land years ago. No one knew how it got there in the first place. The boys hurried towards the ferry.

They were stopped in their tracks when a donut-shaped ball flew into view. As it came closer, it hovered towards Nathaniel, like an uninvited guest.

"I know what this is. It is a biometric drone made by Adrian Lightwood. Maybe there is a lot more suspense hidden from the time Nathaniel received his powers till this moment…" Kamran's voice trailed off as he stared at the flying ball in awe.

"Umm, so what comes next? I am getting goosebumps!!!" Pearce was pacing up and down.

"Hold your horses, Pearce, we have no freaking clue of what is going to happen next. I am still processing this drone/UFO…not sure what to call it" Raymond shook his head.

Nathaniel was reminded of Ria and how annoyed she used to get whenever he and Raymond got over-excited.

"Fine, it may be a biometric drone which is trying to identify me but for who and why? seriously, what is next? As we all take baby steps towards the answer, my curiosity is increasing by the minute," Nathaniel said.

"You boys be curious and excited, but I am on Raymond's side. I want to know what the heck is going on. What if danger lies ahead instead of a pleasant surprise," Kamran quipped.

Raymond and Nathaniel both looked at each other without even knowing what lay ahead. They had already lost Ria, and so, did not need another nasty shock.

"Guys, this is not the right time or place to act like a couple. Rather focus on a new situation that is hurling towards us. There is something very sinister going on, Said Kamran as he pointed his trembling hand toward an enormous robot.

The boys turned around in the direction Kamran was pointing and immediately went cold.

There in front of them was a giant robot almost 100 ft in height. It looked like someone had haphazardly painted blue, red, and golden brown on it. It stood without moving, and then there was a whirring sound. A panel opened on its right leg revealing an empty space. The boys walked closer to the entrance of the panel to see what was inside.

They noticed that the empty space inside the panel appeared almost like a small room. As if it was some sort of a control center. In the control center, there was this huge screen on one of the walls. As they were curiously staring at the screen, suddenly a recording started playing and a face showed up on the screen.

"Hi boys. Welcome to the control center of Xandacross. I have been expecting you boys for a while now. Hi Nathanial, so you are the technopath of this group. Nice job in leading your team to me! You all might be wondering who I am? I am Adrian Lightwood, and this robot is an invention of mine. Look, down below the screen and you will see four hoverboards, four armlets, and four watches. The armlets are detectors and controllers. They detect any threat from evil forces and can be also used to control the level of attack that you would want to execute using the Robot on your enemies. The watches help you to specify the type of attack, they also have super barriers which can block any weapon and its attack in the world, even the most dangerous ones. The watches also have a teleportation ability, if anytime you want to teleport yourself here or any other location on this planet, just command the watch. The watches can also function as an advanced medical scanner which can easily detect any internal injuries to any part of the body and can recommend the cure. It can also monitor the recovery from any injury and alert if there is any risk to life" Adrian spoke with a smile on his face.

The boys took the armlets, watches, and hoverboards. As they picked up the accessories, they saw a strange looking Glove lying on another glass compartment next to these three accessories. Adrian had not mentioned anything about the Glove so they boys wondered what it was for, however they left it behind.

Adrian's voice continued, "The high – tech glove that you all see in that glass compartment helps the technopath to operate the arm movements of the robot and it can sometime suggest the best attack to the technopath to defeat a monster. And not to forget, there is a red button on the glove, which when pressed camouflages the Glove and it becomes invisible to everyone other than the person who wears it." Nathaniel took the glove and pressed the red button.

"Lastly, the hoverboards help all of you to fly the robot. Wait, where is the poison-blooded member of your team? You all are missing an important member of your team. The boys looked at each other puzzled. They wondered, who was Adrian talking about?

Now listen up, I am going to tell something important. You all must be wondering, why am I giving you all these powers. Well, I have been monitoring you boys for few years now. I have selected you all for a special cause. Our world as you know is soon going to be threatened by a dangerous organization headed by a notorious criminal who is planning to wipe out the entire humanity and create his own world of demons and nocturnal creatures. So, your team's mission is to thwart all the evil attacks of this dangerous criminal and eventually destroy him and his organization. From now, you all will be known as the "**Tech Teens**". Goodbye boys and good luck! By the way, please do make sure to read the manuals in detail to know more about all the attacks and defense and other features of the accessories. With this, Adrian's face disappeared from the screen.

The Tech Teens spent some more time in the control panel of the Robot, reading the manuals and familiarizing themselves with all the attacks and defense mechanisms available to them.

As darkness fell, the boys decided that it was best that they returned home before their parents got worried about them and started searching for them. They left the place, thinking who 'Poison – Blooded' was? And when they will have their first encounter with the missing member of their team.

***

Chapter 2 – An Awkward Introduction.

The Video of Adrian Lightwood Left Everyone in Confusion. It was Time to Move from Confusion to an Awkward Introduction.

What happened? Did the teens stumble on to their fate, or did fate come knocking at their door? The events that were unfolding were becoming more and more tangled and messing up the thinking process of the boys.

***

"I am still struggling to understand two crucial aspects of this Robot from the video – "Poison-blooded" and the "Hidden truth", what are they? Nathaniel scratched his head in confusion.

"I guess you are under too much strain. Give it a break, dear brother. The more you think about it, the more it will be difficult to untangle these threads of questions."

"Yeah, but then the video has left us all thinking. Oh yes, and not to forget that it has been three months since Ria's passing, and now danger has knocked on our door. Where do all these findings lead us to? Nathaniel said.

"All I know is this. We somehow need to find out who this co-pilot is. But can we please stop fretting about this for the moment, and let's go down for dinner."

***

"Come on, boys. I do not like serving cold dinner. I want to see both of you at the table on the count of three," Mariah smiled.

The boys rushed down the creaky old stairs. As they took each step, it felt as the stairs were groaning in pain.

As Nathaniel took a seat, he said, "These stairs are groaning quite a bit these days. They are so old. I wonder how old this house is?"

"Shut up Nathaniel, who said that this house is old? It still looks so new like, we have just moved in yesterday," Raymond winked at Nathaniel.

"Okay, point noted. But I must ask one crucial question, tomorrow, do we have to submit any homework?"

"Nope, according to my sharp memory, we don't have any homework. Yeah, but we have a newbie joining us."

"Oh, tell me about this newbie. What do you know about him/her?" Mariah was curious as she passed the salad bowl to Raymond.

"Mum, the newbie, is a girl…her name is Ria Walker," Nathaniel could not bear to look at Mariah.

"Oh, the name and surname are exactly like our daughter's. I wonder if she looks just like our Ria", said Mariah with a twinkle in her eyes.

There was a sudden chill in the room. Hearing Ria's name forced the Walker's to recall their previous life when their sis Ria was alive. Ria was such a darling. She was someone people would never forget, and now it seemed as she was going to make a re-entry into their lives.

"Why? Wasn't it you who ran to the boys' room and cried your heart out when the principal first informed us that a student by the name of Ria Walker would be joining our school?" Nathaniel rolled his eyes.

"Yeah, that was me. But my heart says that this newbie and our sis look alike. Exactly a copy of each other. How would you answer that?", said Raymond.

"I don't know, but if your prediction is accurate, then we may be able to reunite with our sis", replied Nathaniel with much anticipation.

"That is enough! Why don't you two accept the truth that Ria is dead? Don't give yourself false hopes which might later shatter your heart like glass when it falls to the ground."

Mariah stood up and pushed her chair back. She stormed out and walked to her room, slamming the door shut. She was miserable after they lost the apple of their eye. She sat at the edge of the bed, tears streaming and her mind silently screaming.

"Why? Why did you have to leave your mother like this, honey? It feels my life is over..." This sentence kept playing like a loop in her mind. If only her sons knew how truly tormented, she was.

"I am not feeling like eating as my stomach is churning with curiosity," said Raymond.

"So have I", said Nathaniel.

Raymond felt vulnerable. He couldn't stop thinking about the day when the tragic incident took their sister away from them. To date, all that the police could tell them was that it was a hit and run case. They were still trying to find the driver and the car.

Nathaniel got up and walked up the stairs to his room. As he entered his room, his eyes caught the rusty old frame lying on his bedside table. He picked up the frame and held it close to his chest.

Raymond knocked on Nathaniel's door, but there was no answer. He gently opened the door and peeked in. Nathaniel was cuddled up with the frame tightly around his arms and had closed his eyes. Raymond gently shut the door behind him.

***

"Good morning. Nath, wake up. Your brother is waiting for you downstairs. Uhmm..." Mariah did not complete her sentence for some reason.

Nathaniel rubbed his sleepy eyes and said, "What is it, mum? You look stressed?

"Sorry about last night. I should have controlled my anger. I saw the look on your face and your interest in knowing more about the newbie."

"I know, but maybe you are correct as well. I am also sorry."

Mother and son hugged each other. Mariah smiled.

***

"Good morning Nath and Ray!!!!" Kamran waved at the brothers.

"Hey, guys! Sorry, I am late because I have been working on this stupid homework given by my tutor," Pearce frowned.

"Right now, I don't care about your tuition problems; I am interested in that newbie who is joining us today," Nathaniel said.

"As your neighbor, I could hear Mrs. Walker shout at you guys yesterday. I can only imagine how much this continues to hurt the family," Kamran shrugged.

"Yeah, I feel sorry for you guys too, but hold yourselves together and face the future boldly," Pearce had to add his two cents worth.

While the brothers were receiving lessons on being courageous, someone cut across the group.

"Hey! Oh gosh, darn it! On my first day, and I must face idiots? But anyway, uhm…" The voice sounded very familiar.

The boys stared at this rude intruder. Her hair looked familiar. The voice had the same softness and harshness at the same time.

Nathaniel bravely asked, "Are you the new student?"

"Yeah, I am, but how did you guys know? I have known all of you for an exceptionally long time," the stranger replied, scanning the boy's faces.

Kamran and Pearce had the same thought, *"Who is this person? She has made us skip a heartbeat."*

"Those small hands, black gloves, green eyes, and those Chinese dragon on those snow-white cheeks…it had to be her…she looks so familiar…has god responded to our call?" Nathaniel wondered.

"What is your name," Raymond asked. He knew but wanted to hear her say it.

"My name is Ria Walker. I am a transfer student from another school. I hope we can be incredibly good friends."

Nathaniel wanted to ask her to repeat her name, but he had heard it loud and clear. His heart was racing. It seemed his sadness had disappeared momentarily.

"Nice to meet your Ria. Do you want to join our group?" Nathaniel asked.

"I know the name of your group, "THE TECH TEENS" right?"

"But… how do you know? I mean, you are new here, right?" Raymond had a puzzled look on his face.

"I was a student here before I moved to Chicago about few months back".

"I have special powers too." Ria winked at the boys. She was breaking into a cold sweat. She had to watch her tongue.

"When did you move to Chicago?" Nathaniel was curious.

"I transferred on 13th July…"

Nathaniel looked at Raymond. Was this a mere coincidence? They were baffled because the same day their sis Ria had breathed her last in the hospital right before their eyes.

Kamran extended his right hand, "Hi, I am Kamran Coyle, their best friend,"

"Hi, I am Pearce Ames, their best friend too."

"Hmm… I assume that we all are in the same class. So, mind helping me locate the classroom?" asked Ria.

Pearce pointed the way as they walked towards the classroom.

"Why do I get the feeling that there is something mysterious about this girl Ria Walker," Nathaniel thought as he observed Ria.

"Nathaniel, is everything alright?" Ria asked.

"Yeah…"

"Then come on…"

***

"Wait!? What! Ria, Ria Walker, how come you are back? I thought you were dead. Is this a miracle?" David asked Nathaniel and his companies in a low tone as they entered the classroom with Ria.

"Excuse me, Ria Walker. Hey, weren't you dead?" Suzy asked, flipping her hair to one side.

"Oh Gosh! Stop it. I am new here. Also, who claimed I'm dead? I am a transfer student from another school", exclaimed Ria.

"Guys, she is the new student. She is an exact lookalike of sis." Nathaniel had a wide grin.

"Guys, quick, let's be seated before Ms. Angela arrives. I think she is going to explode when she sees Ria," Raymond chuckled.

The classroom was a buzz. Ria was talking to her classmates as if she never left. She was so comfortable in this environment.

"Good morning. Wait! How is this possible? Am I daydreaming? Ria Walker, is that you? You, you are alive," Ms. Angela asked nervously.

"I am sorry miss; I have no idea who you are talking about? I am the new transfer student." Replied Ria.

Ms. Angela interrupted her, "Oh, Okay! Anyways, we all must be nice to this newbie and help her settle in. Okay? Please sit, Ria!"

Angela's last sentence explained how flabbergasted she was to see Ria Walker.

Miss. Angela asked, "What was the topic we covered last class? Anyone?"

Ria raised her hand, "Story writing, I guess."

Angela frowned. She tried hard not to show her frustration.

"How did you know that?" questioned Miss. Angela.

"I recalled seeing the weekly schedule, and it showed that last week you taught them story writing.", replied Ria.

Angela controlled her anger and let out a smile. This Ria was sharp, just like the previous Ria.

"Wow, you have a strong memory. But can you please tell me one thing, when did you check the weekly subject schedule?" questioned Miss. Angela.

"I checked the schedule a week ago when I visited the school before joining, and I saw the schedule of this class outside the subject schedule board. I had taken a picture of it.", replied Ria.

Ms. Angela smiled, and the lesson began. The next hour went without incident. At the back of her mind, Angela felt an uneasiness which she was unable to shake off. She had this undeniable conviction that Ria Walker had arisen from the dead.

The bell rang, and the class was dismissed.

***

As the students walked out of class, Nathaniel thought, *"She has the same intelligence as Kamran and my sis. I guess*

Ray's predictions were accurate, but I still have so many unanswered questions."

"Oh my god! Ria, you were amazing, I am gob smacked the way you answered all those questions. I mean, how do you do it? You are so confident," Raymond beamed.

"I am starving. Can we all please go and eat something in the canteen? The rats are playing rugby and baseball in my stomach," Pearce rubbed his tummy.

"Ditto, I am starving," Kamran added.

"Okay! Let's grab something to eat and then head for the cherry blossom garden. The weather is awesome today, so we can eat there." Raymond replied.

"Uhm, you guys move ahead. I want to go to the washroom, keep my books in my locker, and then I will join you, people, at the garden directly," Ria quipped and started to walk away from the group.

"Sure, but take care of yourself and beware of the other students, they all are jerks!" Nathaniel winked at Ria.

***

Ria thought, *"Okay, it was weird to enter the washroom, the way those girls were staring at me. Why should I stick my nose in their business, anyway?"*

Ria was not so thrilled at the idea of going to the garden. Her stomach was churning, and her mind was swirling. But she had no excuse, so she made her way to the garden. She loved it in autumn when the trees shed the blossoms.

She sat beside Kamran and started singing.

"I am a fighter, dancing in the fire, hoping to fly higher, above the horizon reaching the heaven…."

"Hang on…how do you know that song? That is an incredibly special song sung by Circuit Beats," Nathaniel stared at Ria in disbelief.

"Oh yeah, the name of this song is "True to You." I always listen to it when I have conflicts in my mind. It soothes me," Pearce said.

"Not exactly... but yeah, this song is so inspirational," Kamran added.

"This song was Sis's favorite. She used to sing it every time when she used to sit on the roof under a starry night," Raymond was reminiscing.

The teens were amazed. This girl had just entered their lives less than two hours ago, and she seemed to fit like a glove. It felt as if their sister Ria had only left them temporarily.

Ria suddenly got up and walked towards the lake, that was covered in a blanket of baby pink leaves. A few steps were leading towards the water and she took two steps and sat down.

"What's wrong with her?" Nathaniel wondered.

The boys walked towards Ria. As they got closer, they could hear a soft sob.

"What's wrong? Was there something I said which offended you? Raymond asked.

"No, everything is alright. I recalled something from my past. Which made me sad.", replied Ria.

The boys thought they were one step closer to finding out the truth, but Ria wiped out their memory with her magic and skipped the time between the bitter truth and lunch.

***

"It feels like a rock hit me because I cannot even recall how fast the lunch break ended," Nathaniel shook his head.

"Okay, let's get some physical education. Let's go to the field," Raymond said.

"Ria, are you excited about physical education lecture? Huh!? Where did Ria go?" Kamran looked around. Ria was nowhere in sight.

"Wasn't she behind us, listening to our conversation? Where did she go," Pearce asked.

"I bet it is that jerk, Jacky. I bet he is trying to make trouble. We must find Ria," Nathaniel started looking around for Ria. The boys followed.

***

"You better get your priorities straight, and who are you to boss around me? I mean, what rights do you have? Back off!" Ria stormed at Jacky.

"Oh! Look who is showing her attitude to the great leader of the seniors! I mean, who are you to talk to me so arrogantly?" Jacky looked at Ria with menacing eyes.

"Take this puny little Jerk!" Jacky pushed Ria against the locker door.

Nathaniel and the others could hear loud bangs coming from the locker area and rushed towards the sound. They were scared for Ria. Hopefully, she was not hurt.

"Guys, I guess that jerk is taking our buddy down, and she is not responding the same way because she does not want to get into a fight on her first day.

Jacky, what do you think you are doing? Let go of her! Better not mess with the pro-wrestling champion Pearce Ames! Get that!?"

"Let go off her! I hope you know that I have a special relationship with the school's chairman. If I desire, I can have you expelled from school!" Kamran roared in anger.

"Stop, guys! Please, I don't want any ruckus or damage here," Ria straightened herself.

"We are just upset. Give us the signal, and we will beat the hell out of Jacky. Oh, we will hurt him bad. Look, we hate seeing you like this on your first day at college, and especially when Raymond and I feel a special connection to you," Nathaniel had a look of concern.

"Yeah, the positive vibe which we feel when you are around is special. It feels like you are a part of our family," Raymond added.

"Thank you for your show of support and concern. I am a strong girl, and I can take care of myself. There is no point in getting into a fight with a jerk like Jacky and getting your hands dirty and ending up in detention. It's just not worth it."

Ria turned to Jacky and said, "I guess now I know why they call you a "JERK", because of your arrogance and attitude."

Suddenly, she swung her fist and brought it towards Jacky's nose. She stopped an inch away. The look of terror on Jacky's face was priceless. Ria was done here. The boy's jaws dropped as they saw Ria's classy act.

"Look, if I am sweet and cute one moment, the other moment, I might be your worst nightmare coming to life in daylight. So, stay away is my suggestion."

Jacky sneered, "I will ensure that you are thrown out of the school, and at that time, there will be no scope for your return Walker! That's my promise."

"Ria! Jacky!"

That was principal Jack calling their names from behind. He was taking long strides towards them, and there was a look of disgust on his face. He stopped in front of Jacky and Ria. The boys moved to the side. Kamran was slightly shaking, and Raymond grabbed his shoulder to calm him down.

"Sir, I gladly accept any punishment, but before you do, you must know that Jacky is the one who started all of this ruckus...."

"Who said I am going to punish you?". Principal Jack said as he cut Ria off mid-sentence.

"What really happened here Kamran?", Principle Jack asked Kamran.

"This was all started by Jacky. He was trying to boss around Ria as she is a new student and today is her first day in our school", replied Kamran with a honest look in his eyes.

"Is that so?", Principal Jack angrily looked at Jacky as he saw his son quietly staring at the floor.

"Knowing that his father was really angry and there was no way he could have lied as there were eye-witnesses to the whole incident who would happily support Ria", Jacky accepted that he was the culprit.

Principal Jack looked visibly upset, and before he walked off, Jacky had received a two-weeks suspension. Principal Jack was highly embarrassed that his son was nowhere the ideal son he had hoped him to be.

"Let us take you to first aid. Look at that nasty bruise Jacky gave you on your arm by pressing his fingers so firmly onto your soft flesh as he hurled you towards the locker." Nathaniel pointed to Ria's arm.

Ria smiled and muttered some strange words which sounded like a magical spell.... REPARICA... %%%###$$$$." The very next moment the bruise from Ria's hand had vanished as if it never existed.

"You are a magician!" exclaimed Kamran.

Nathaniel thought to himself, *"Woah! This sounded like the same strange spell that sis used whenever she was injured. My suspicions are slowly getting some roots. There is an uncanny resemblance between this new student and my sis Ria."*

Suddenly a loud roar distracted the boy's attention. They looked around in panic but could not see what had created that loud sound. The sound appeared to have originated from a distant location and not the college campus. They boys looked at Ria, but she appeared to be normal as if she had not heard anything. Oh, no, it had been two months since they had discovered the robot and the Adrian Lightwood's video. It was a signal for the boys to head towards the robot. They looked at each other.

Raymond was the first to speak.

"Uhm... Ria, we must go, so let's see each other later."

The boys ran out of the corridors flying out of the doors and rushed to where their cycles had been parked. Ria smiled as if she knew where the boys were headed to.

***

At the Forbidden Ferry, they found the robot waiting for them. Its monolithic structure stood against the ghastly desolate backdrop. The boys walked up to the entrance of the robot. A panel slid open, and the boys sort their hoverboards.

They boys had been instructed by Adrian's video that they were selected to form a special tech team to battle monsters and other villains from time to time to save the earth and its people from catastrophic dangers.

***

Few minutes later the Tech Teens reached at their first battle site. The team and the robot came flying through the clear sky and everyone used their camouflage mode to hide their presence from people.

"Pearce, use the ice plasma punch!!" Nathaniel yelled.

"IPP, coming right up!" Pearce replied as he typed on his watch the attack name.

Today, the battle was with a four-legged freak. It looked like a human for the most part, except on closer inspection, it was made up of thousands of tiny dots, to be precise, metal dots. As the boys maneuvered and tried to destroy the monster, it would magically rebuild itself, and so this battle went on for a few hours. The boys attacked with a wide range of their hoverboard, armlets, and watches however, they were unable to destroy the monster. Soon, the boys started to worry that they were going to lose the battle as the monster kept coming back at them with one after other more powerful attacks. At this very moment Nathaniel wished that her sister was alive to bail them out of their first losing battle.

***

At school, Ria sat under one of the cherry blossoms trees. As the wind blew, a few petals fell on her. Ria picked one up and looked at it and instantly knew that Nathaniel, Raymond and their friends were fighting a losing battle against a dangerous monster. She wanted to help but knew that this was not the right time to intervene and reveal everything. She had to wait a little longer for the right time. She closed her eyes and her Chinese dragon mark begin to glow. She was on her way to be teleported to the battle scene.

***

"Oh god, the right arm of our robot is irreparably damaged. It looks like the robot has taken a fair beating today." Nathaniel was not happy at all.

"I cannot help right now. We are still in the middle of a fierce battle. I can fix it only after this battle is over. We desperately need some help today to defeat this monster". Raymond lamented.

***

"YOU! You 4-legged freak come over here". Nathaniel and his friends suddenly heard Ria's voice, challenging the monster.

The Tech Teens were totally shocked to see Ria appear from nowhere at the battle scene. "Ria, what are you doing here? How did you locate us? why are you joining in our fight? This is very risky. Please stay out of this", Nathaniel was becoming edgy.

"What is she trying to do anyway? Does she have powers to fight monsters like us? Pearce boldly asked.

"I must circle the outdoor fountain manufacturer twice to distract this freak so that I can gain some time to prepare my special attack," Ria started circling around with her high speed skates.

She was not worried about facing the challenge. It was like fighting a war without weapons, yet it was a matter of prestige.

"What on earth is she up to? Is she playing with the monster, or is it the other way round? I bet these two are playing rather than fighting with each, it feels the dog and owner are playing but who is the dog and who is the owner?" Raymond chuckled.

"Can't you understand what she is trying to do? She is trying to confuse the poor thing. If it cannot catch Ria, it will be shameful. Let' leave the sentiments out, it's just a monster," Kamran laughed as he watched on in amusement.

"Guys, just shut up and watch the fun," Pearce was having fun.

"Yes, all in to watch this small film filled with action, rather than suspense," Nathaniel laughed.

"Okay, here I go. Finally, the monster has fallen into my illusion trap. Now all I need to do is gather all my strength to destroy it!", Ria exclaimed.

"So far, Ria has amazed us with her presence of mind and powers but now I wonder what else she has up her sleeves to amaze us. All I hope is she does not harm herself," Nathaniel smiled nervously.

Ria could sense Nathaniel's concern and fear for her. But she knew this was not the time to get bogged down with emotions as even a minute of distraction could be fatal for her as well as her friends. She needed to first finish off this monster once and for all.

"Guys, did you notice the change in Ria's expression. It feels like she is lost in some thoughts. I hope she comes out of it soon and launches her final deadly attack on this monster. We cannot hold off this monster for too long as it seems be becoming stronger and stronger with every passing minute" Nathaniel remarked.

"Concentrate," Ria told herself. She had to put her thoughts aside and focus on defeating the threat. She had to fulfill her duty as a friend.

Ria shouted, "You four–legged freak, how dare you attack my friends, now you shall pay, RAINBOW SOLAR BEAM!!"

This was the ultimate attack. It drained all of Ria's energy, and she went white. It was worth the risk. The monster disintegrated, and a small hole opened in the ground swallowing all the remnants of the beast. With a roar, the ground closed. All traces of the monster vanished.

Nathaniel and Raymond were both speechless after the spectacle they witnessed. They once again were dawn back to their memory banks. What was the origin of these attacks?

Ria fell to the ground. It seemed all the energy had been drained from her body.

"Ria, Woah! She has fainted. Ray and Kamran, please go and get Ria. We must scan her for any signs of injury. Now!!!!" Nathaniel said.

Raymond and Kamran gently helped Ria get back on to her feet. Ria opened her eyes and smiled weakly.

"Kamran is she okay? Is there any sign of injury?" Pearce asked with a look of dread on his face.

"All her vital signs are okay. There is nothing to be worried about. I mean, her body has taken a beating considering she used a lot of energy to pull that off. Give her few minutes, and she will regain the color in her cheeks.", Kamran chuckled.

***

"Uhm… Where on earth am I? it feels as if I ran 200 miles today. Wait, Nathaniel, Pearce, Raymond & Kamran, what are you guys doing here?"

"Welcome back to earth," Nathaniel smiled.

"How do you feel?" Kamran asked.

"What's up with you guys today? Why are you guys being so emotional? It is beginning to annoy me." Ria asked.

"But, with what motive did you use that attack? And who taught you that attack?" Raymond was curious.

"Oh, my motive was to save you all, and I never learned it. Instead, I was born with the spell. I have magical powers," Ria said quietly.

"Hey, do you want to come home and grab the notes you missed last week because that was our first week at college," Nathaniel asked out of the blue.

"Sure," Ria replied.

Both Nathaniel and Raymond jumped in and said, "Woah, take it easy, you are still weak,"

Ria got up and looked around. "What is this place?"

The boys looked at each other and shook their heads. Ria, I think we should leave it here for now. There is too much to share. Right now, we need to take you home. You need to rest.

***

"I hope you will love our home," Nathaniel smiled.

"Mum, we are back! I guess she is not home yet!" Raymond scanned the living area and the kitchen.

"Hello boys, I will be down in a second." Mariah shouted from upstairs.

There was an air of excitement in Mariah's voice. Both Nathaniel and Raymond wondered why.

"Did you notice how happy mum is sounding today? She has not sounded like this in a long time," Nathaniel smiled as he said this.

Ria was lost in her thoughts as she stared at a frame resembling her,

"Ria, why are you staring at that frame like that? You look so cute when you stare at something like that. You remind me of my sister, Ria," Nathaniel joked.

"Yeah, you look exactly like our sis at this moment. It made us recall for a moment how our sis used to stare at an object," Raymond added.

"You are something special, Ria Walker," Pearce said.

"You are a great friend as well. Why do we sound so nostalgic suddenly?" Kamran added.

"Correction. Not nostalgic, instead, weird, and formal. What made you guys start talking like that? I mean it is super eerie".

"Welcome home, boys! How was your day?" Mariah asked while walking down the stairs.

"It was amazing, nothing like other days. It was a day to remember with this new friend of ours who joined our school today. I would like to introduce to you Ria Walker," Nathaniel pointed towards Ria.

Mariah's eyes lit up. There was Ria Walker, smiling at her. For a moment Mariah felt her own daughter was standing right in front of her.

"Okay, boys, there is something that I have never shared with you guys. Look properly at your friend Ria's neck. Can you see the black heart on her neck?"

The boys thought that Mariah was probably in shock and was seeing their friend Ria as her own daughter whom she had lost just few months back. They chuckled but noticed Mariah was standing stone-faced. Her expression had not changed.

"Mrs. Walker, do you mean the birthmark which Nathaniel has on his neck? Our friend Ria had it too," Pearce said.

"Wait, mum, what are you trying to say?" Nathaniel asked looking completely surprised.

"Yes, both Nathaniel and Ria had the same birth mark on their neck", how can I ever forget that. Mariah said, still inspecting the birth mark on Ria's neck.

Suddenly Ria addresses Mariah, as "Mum". Hearing that word from Ria's mouth, everyone in the room felt as if they were struck by lightning when Ria Walker said this word.

"What? What did you just say? Repeat it," Raymond asked. He had a shocked expression.

"Does that mean you are our sister Ria Walker?" Nathaniel asked excitedly.

"Yes. Okay, let me show you the birthmark if you don't believe me."

Ria snapped her finger, and a birthmark appeared on her neck. Ria's family reunion was underway.

"Wait, Ria, was it you all along? Kamran asked.

"Look, I have the same mark as Nathaniel. Yes, it was me all along. I was with you all the entire day even without you noticing my real identity. Although, we had a few close calls."

Happy tears now started flowing. Mariah hugged Ria tightly, and then there was a tug of war as to who would hug her next. It was a very happy reunion.

"Sis, how did we not recognize you?" Nathaniel was confused.

"This has to have been the best awkward introduction," Raymond yelled in happiness.

"I also have another secret which I cannot share in front of you mum. I hope you understand." Ria looked at Mariah and smiled.

"Yeah, go ahead and share with your brothers while I prepare some snacks for all of you," Mariah walked towards the kitchen.

Once she was out of sight, Ria whispered, "Guys, I know the Robot you all met the other day. His name is Xandacross. I know how to activate all the power and strikes of Xandacross. I know all of its features. You can pretty much say that I am his owner.

"What!? Oh my god, I guess I must now run out to the middle of the road and scream my lungs out," Nathaniel was beside himself.

"You better not do that; I will not spare you."

Nonetheless, the awkward introduction made this ordinary reunion the most memorable one for all.

Chapter 3 – The Start of Heroism

Their Happiness held no Bound. The Siblings were Back. The Trio, the Triplets – All One Again.

The Walker brothers and their mother circled the bonfire, recalling the sweet memories. For the first time in a long time, all their faces were lit, their hearts were light, and their conversations a fun.

"And then, that jerk was like, "I am sorry Nathaniel, please let go of me. I beg you". Nathaniel burst out laughing.

"That's right do not pick up a fight with Nathaniel Sir," Nathaniel added.

"Oh yeah, I recall that incident now, but what sis did today was also amazing. The way she brought her fist so close to Jacky, and left the fist inches from his face... I bet she would have broken his nose," Raymond chuckled.

"Where is Ria?" Mariah wondered.

"She is probably on the roof lying down and counting the stars and planning some mischief or waiting for us to come and be with her? For we are her brothers after all," Nathaniel winked.

"I suggest you go and see what she is up to," Mariah smiled.

Raymond and Nathaniel got up and walked up close to the bonfire. They warmed their hands and headed to the back of the house. There was a ladder propped against the back wall. The brothers took turns to climb up the ladder to Ria and greet the night sky.

***

"Sis, Woah! Climbing up this roof is like climbing Mount Everest. Ah! At last, Nathaniel Dave Walker has achieved his goal and reached the peak of Mount Everest to meet his sister who had the patience to wait for him at the peak."

"Congratulations! Raymond Dave Walker. He has also achieved his goal by accompanying his younger brother, helping him reach the peak, and meeting up with his sister."

"I, Ria Walker feel proud to be Mariah Walker's daughter, and Nathaniel and Raymond Walker's sister. I am grateful to be your sister."

This moment was a magical moment. The Walker siblings had never felt so connected like they felt this evening.

"Sis, why are you here all alone? I mean, watching the stars is fun, but it also fun down there by the fire. Brrr! It is freezing up here," Nathaniel rubbed his hands.

"I know, yet nothing can beat the view of the magical skyline. Look at the carpet of stars as far as your eyes can see them. Besides, I feel as if there are a lot of memories attached here, up on the roof."

"Woah, look a shooting star. Let us make a wish!" Raymond pointed to the sky.

That one shooting knew so much, more than any other star in the sky. It held the memories and the wishes of the siblings. Who knew that just one star could contain so much?

"Ria, please start from the beginning. What happened on the day of the accident?" Nathaniel asked.

"Okay, Sure I can tell you what really happened but just so that you both know, I only remember faintly and what I felt, or experienced may seem weird to both of you. Ria remarked". She continued, while the surgeon was busy trying to save me, I felt I was already dead. I suddenly felt as if I had left my body and had travelled to a divine plane. There, I hovered over a white sofa when a figure appeared in front of me. I was told that an evil force had organized that car crash on purpose to kill me. Apparently, I possess magical powers. I have had them since childhood but never knew I had them. The figure explained that some evil force was lurking in on earth, and I was the apparent savior. When the time came, a divine being would activate my powers. A sample of that is what I demonstrated today, during the fight with the monster."

"Yes, you are right Ria, I am sorry, but this is quite an amusing story. It is hard to believe because it is like you had a brief afterlife or sorts after you died. It is hard to believe such stuff even coming from you sis. But anyway, where were you the last three months. In that plane?" Raymond scratched his head.

"Yes, my soul kept hovering over that white sofa for those three months. I was in a state of suspension, but it was pure bliss. No pain, no affliction. I felt nothing but serenity. Until yesterday, when the figure appeared and said it was time for me to go back to my body and fulfil my mission as a savior."

There was silence for a few minutes as Nathaniel and Raymond tried to reconcile with this information. The brothers wished that no new threat would ever come to their sister and she would always remain close to them. Ria wished that she could always protect her family, friends, and the entire world from any threats which lurked around.

Suddenly, Ria looked at her brothers with a panic-stricken face and said, "I cannot feel my right leg."

"What!?" Raymond and Nathaniel both shouted at the same time.

"I cannot feel my right leg. It is numb. What should I do?"

"Try moving your leg. It should help," Raymond shrugged.

"Just try to move it left or right. Oh god, how did it happen?" Nathaniel added.

"Ouch, it is tough to move it with force, but yeah, I can move it a bit. It is tough, though."

"Oh, thank god. I think you have been sitting out here for too long. It is freezing up here," Nathaniel said.

"Yeah, I think the same as well. It is nothing so serious, it will be okay within five minutes. But I think we should go in. It is warmer in the house," Raymond said.

"Okay, but I want to stay up here for a few minutes more," Ria said. She pulled her knees up to her chest and bent over to hug them.

This was the beginning of a new threat. The numbness was disappearing, but the danger was just around the corner. Ria remembered that she was struck with the same numbness attack the day before. She tried to move her leg again.

Ria panicked in her mind, *"What is happening to me? Why isn't it working? I should try again, it will go away. This numbness will disappear. Ouch, it is hurting so much when I force any movement."*

Ria tried once more and was successful this time but was overly concerned with her previous failed attempts.

Ria reminded herself, *"I feel much better, but I must keep it a secret as I do not want anyone to be bothered with this minor issue, nor will I be bothered. I hope it is just a poor circulation and not really indication of a new threat lurking around."*

Ria stayed up on the roof for a few more minutes, and then she said goodnight to the stars and went down to retire for the day.

***

"Good morning, Ray. Good morning mum, where is sis? She hasn't come down yet."

"You two are seriously something; both woke up, and the first thing you ask is about your sister."

"Why? Does it feel weird, mum?" Nathaniel asked.

"No, I recall the past when you two would come down and start looking for your sister."

"Those were the days, but then we were not ourselves for almost three months. But now, those days are back again in our home," Raymond beamed.

"Stop reminding me of that incident. It gives me goosebumps to imagine it once again," Mum sighed.

"Topic change. Okay, how about we wake sis up?" Nathaniel pointed to the stairs.

"There is no need for that. Ria Walker isn't a kid who needs to be woken up by anyone. She is a mature young lady who is going to be 16 in a few weeks." Ria said, as she hurried down the stairs.

Everyone burst out laughing.

"You look grump today honey, everything alright?"

"Yeah mum, everything is fine. I just bumped my head on the bathroom door, and that made me grumpy, even though it was my fault as I was half asleep, yet I blame that stupid door."

"I second that. The door is worth blaming. Even I banged my head on the door this morning," Raymond said.

Thus, the morning routine began. Mariah made pancakes for breakfast while she could hear her two sons, arguing upstairs who would use the bathroom first. Soon, her thoughts shifted to Ria and how happy she was that Ria was home.

At the breakfast table, Mariah commented, "Nath, Ray, listen, please take care of your sis. I just don't want her to get into any trouble and keep her protected from Jacky."

"Yeah, of course, mum," Nathaniel rolled his eyes.

"Mom!!!"

Hearing that sudden scream alarmed, and they all rushed to Ria's room.

"Nat! Help me! Please, Nat."

"Ria, are you alright? Ria," Mariah asked in a frightened voice.

Witnessing Ria moaning in pain made Mariah's heart sink into an ocean of panic. What was happening to her dear daughter?

"Sis, what happened? Why did you scream suddenly? Is everything okay?" Raymond looked at Ria, who was sitting on her bed.

"Sis, get up!" Nathaniel was screaming now.

"Ah! That's why I screamed. I am unable to feel my leg, just like last night."

Nathaniel felt as if he were about to have a panic attack but pushed those thoughts aside. Instead, he and Raymond aided Ria to get her back on her feet.

"I can barely feel my legs."

"Mum, do you have any medicine that may help Ria with her numbness," Nathaniel asked.

"Wait here. Let me get some medicine that reduces the numbness, but it does not completely cure it; the effect lasts for about twelve hours. But if the numbness returns, take another pill."

"What do you mean again?" Nathaniel looked at Mariah.

"It may happen again. Looking at Ria's condition, there is a good possibility that the issue will return. I will go to the hospital and consult some senior doctors about it, but for now Ria is your responsibility."

Mariah left the room and returned with a bottle of pink pills. She handed one to Nathaniel. He picked up the glass of water on Ria's bedside and gave her the glass. Ria's eyes were now bloodshot.

A few minutes passed.

"How do you feel now, sis? Is it any better?" Nathaniel held Ria's hand.

"How are you feeling now? Has the numbness reduced?" Raymond was now sitting on Ria's bed.

"I am okay but feel weakness due to the numbness. It seems the numbness is draining my energy."

"This is a serious issue. Usually when this happens, people can simply jump or move their leg for some time to reduce the numbness, but if you are feeling week as if you are losing your energy then it is a completely different issue all together," Mariah said. There was a serious look on her face.

"I think she needs a blood test. Could we do it at the hospital, mum? We may be able to figure it out, but I hope mum is fine with that idea," Raymond said.

"Yes, that will be fine. However, it may not be easy to figure out what has happened with her blood test report, it is extremely complicated to figure out. Anyway, I will inform the hospital staff that you are bringing in Ria later this afternoon, after school." Mum said.

"Yes, let's do this, but can we leave for school now because we have already missed our first two lectures, due to me. I am sorry. I should not have called out to all of you and dealt with it on my own rather than bugging all of you." Ria sighed.

"No, if you didn't share this now, it may have got worse in the future," Raymond said.

"Okay, now you all leave for school, and I shall leave for work. Raymond, Nathaniel, help your sister to get up." Mariah quipped as she picked up her purse to go to the hospital.

***

"Hey Kamran, Hey Pearce. What did we miss in the first two lectures?" Nathaniel asked.

"Nothing much, because the teacher was on sick leave, so we played outside, lucky for you three. Anyways, why are you guys late?" Kamran asked, looking at all of them like the headmaster of the school.

"Okay, so this morning Ria came down with her grumpy mode on, and ten minutes before leaving, she went to her room to grab her bag, and then after five seconds, we heard her screaming out for us. So, we went up to her room and saw that she was sitting on her bed, unable to get up. She was complaining of numbness, and then she was crying. She was barely able to move her leg," Raymond narrated the events of the morning.

Raymond and the others turned backed and saw that Ria was still in pain. She was walking at a snail's pace.

"Sis, hurry, let's go. The lecture is about to start," Nathaniel called out to Ria.

"Yeah, you guys carry on. I still feel weak from the attack of numbness. Kamran, Pearce, could I borrow your laboratory journals as I needed to complete the last part of yesterday's project as both my brothers are slow in writing."

"Kamran, Pearce, after this lecture, we are going to Mum's hospital to get Ria's blood test done. We must find out what is causing her numbness because she had the same issue now twice in last two days. The numbness does not seem to be a small issue because apart from the pain, after each incident she is feeling completely drained out of her energy and is hardly able to walk or do anything. She was in so much pain this morning...Raymond's voice choked off as he turned away his face to hide the tears that were starting to roll down his cheeks.

"Should I try to cheer her up? Because she is looking like a withered flower. Let me make her smile and forget the pain at least for some time," Pearce smiled.

Pearce walked over to Ria and shared a joke. She burst out laughing and then Kamran told her a funny incident which happened in the canteen. Ria was all in smiles now.

"Thanks, everyone, it made me feel much better."

"That's what friends are for," Pearce and Kamran blurted out at the same time.

Everyone burst out laughing, and both the Walker brothers reached out to ruffle their sister's boyish hair and succeeded in doing so.

After their lecture ended, they gathered outside the classroom.

"Okay, let's now go to the hospital, meet with mum and get your blood test done and let's hope that the doctors can figure out what is wrong with you," Raymond said.

"I will meet you at the bicycle shed. I want to go to the washroom," Ria said as she walked towards the washroom, that was past the lockers.

***

As Ria made her way out of the washroom, she heard a whisper, "Hello!"

Ria turned towards the direction from where the voice appeared to have come. But there was no one in the hallway. She thought to herself, it must be my imagination.

As Ria headed down the hallway, towards the bicycle shed, she heard the voice again. This time it was much clear and louder and seemed to have come not too far from where she was standing.

Ria was petrified and let out a scream…

"Ray, Kamran, Pearce, Nat. Help me!!!! Brothe…"

Ria collapsed in the deserted hallway. A shadowy figure appeared from nowhere and walked up to Ria, who was lying on the ground motionless.

"HUH, what happened, puny Walker? How do you feel lying vulnerable on the floor with a numb leg? You shall die. I will destroy you today," The shadowy figure lifted his right leg as if it was ready to crush Ria with a mighty blow.

Ria wanted to get up and fight that strange shadowy figure, but she could only stare at it and had no strength to even move, forget about getting up on her feet to fight. She lied on the ground helpless, waiting for the inevitable. The very next moment she heard a voice. It was her brother, Raymond who was calling out her name.

"Ria, are you okay?" Raymond bent down and scooped Ria up, and sat her upright. "Why did you scream out for us? Why are you so scared? It looks like something or someone freaked you out completely and you collapsed out of fright. Wo! Your body is icy cold."

As Ria sat upright, she drooped her head on to Raymond's shoulder. A feeling of disgust crept in. She hated herself at that moment. She was disappointed that she could not fight that shadowy figure. She was in an extremely fragile state of mind.

"Hang in there. You are going to be fine. We are going to quickly take you to the hospital," Nathaniel said.

Raymond picked Ria up in his arms. He decided that going to the hospital was not a good idea. Ria would be better off being treated on Xandacross, the robot. It was better equipped with the latest medical gadgets. He remembered the scanner they had used the last time when Ria fought the monster. Also, he was afraid to take her to the hospital. The last time she was there, she had died, although, the doctors had tried their best, at this moment. An unknown fear of losing his sister again in the hospital prevented Raymond from taking Ria to the hospital.

"Nat, I think I need you to use your special power. We do not have a choice, but I believe that it is best that Ria should be treated on Xandacross. Can you teleport us there?"

Nathaniel remained silent. When they had watched the video on Xandacross, the first time, Adrian Lightwood had given instructions that they could choose one person to be a 'teleporter'. The only condition was that they could use this power up to a dozen times.

"What are you waiting for, Nat? Do it. Teleport us now!" Kamran shouted impatiently.

"Guys, please hurry. There is a thin line of blood flowing from Ria's mouth. I don't know what to do or how to stop the bleeding," Pearce was anxiously trying to stop the blood flow with no success. His white handkerchief was turning crimson red.

Nathaniel muttered, "Xandacross Access."

***

The five of them now appeared on Xandacross. They gently lay Ria on the sofa in the main control room, and Kamran snatched Pearce's bloody handkerchief. He removed the medical scanner from the socket and scanned the handkerchief. Now he waited for the printer to whirr in the background.

Ria was feeling very miserable. She was tired and worse of all, feeling fragile and helpless.

"This is strange. We have not encountered this kind of situation before. It seems only Ria has been targeted with this strange numbness incident. Do you think there is a possibility that this is actually some sort of attack and is intentional?" Raymond asked.

"Ray has a point. Someone or something has chosen not to harm any of us, just Ria. It seems she is their target. So where do all these things lead us to?" Pearce asked. He had a look of concern.

"Someone has done this to Ria, right under our noses and we could not do anything" Kamran said.

"Nat, what do you have to say? Nat, are you with us?" Raymond asked.

The printer started whirring before Nat could answer, and the boys rushed to the printer. The paper read: Check her blood. It is not reaching the heart.

The boys raced back to Ria.

"Everyone, look at Ria's blood flow. It has a thin rainbow-colored line running through her veins, but the flow is slow, and it is unable to reach her heart," Nathaniel said. He pointed to the flow of blood.

"Nat, do you recall what we learned in science two weeks ago? The heart needs electricity to make it beat, and due to the numbness in Ria's body, it cannot conduct electricity. You can use your technopathic powers to do so," Kamran stated.

Ria closed her eyes. She had fainted. The boys yelled out curses in frustration. Nathaniel closed his eyes and used his power and jolted Ria's heart. He then ran the scanner through her body. A few minutes later, the printer confirmed: Patient is in recovery mode. Body function is normal.

Ria stirred. She slowly opened her eyes and smiled weakly. Nathaniel sat her upright and cuddled her.

"Welcome back Ria."

The boys all came closer. There was a look of relief on all their faces. This was a close call.

"How do you feel? And why did you collapse like that in school?" Raymond quizzed Ria.

"Were you attacked? Or were you feeling anything unusual?" Pearce added.

"Ria, say something. What happened back there? Were you attacked?" Kamran asked.

"Everyone, stop bombarding her and at least let her speak," Nathaniel said. His voice had a ring of irritation to it.

"All I can recall is this, once I came out of the washroom, I suddenly felt weak and could walk only two steps, but when I took my first step I was again attacked by numbness, and this time, I was paralyzed, and my heart stopped beating. I collapsed."

"So, how do you feel now? Are you still feeling the same?" Nathaniel asked.

"I am just weak. The numbness seems to be getting worse, but other than that, I am fine. Wait, don't tell me that you figured out everything already?"

"Don't worry, figuring out your DNA is like figuring out what clothes to wear," Raymond chuckled.

"HA! Hilarious, brother. But seriously, there is one more thing I sensed when I was in my semi-conscious state. There was a gigantic shadow, and it said, "HUH, what happened, puny Walker? How do you feel lying vulnerable on the floor with a numb leg? You shall die today. I will destroy you today. I felt the voice was familiar."

What was happening? Was it someone in Ria's close circle of friends who was after her life, or was there someone else, unknown to all, waiting and planning the next attack on Ria?

Chapter 4 – Numbness Poison

Just as they were Ready to Embrace and Live Normally with Ria, this Poison Attack Proved, this was not the Case. Evil was Lurking Around, Waiting to Strike Again.

Raymond brushed his hands over Ria's hair. He was concerned. This was not good. Ria looked deathly pale even though she was attempting to put up a brave front. All he could do was comfort her with some kind words. He did not want to hear another moan or scream. It was unbearable to see his sister suffer like this.

"Ria, you might feel a pinch as I inject the needle in your arm to take blood sample for testing. So, if you feel anything at all, just don't scream out," Raymond said.

Ria was a tough cookie. A needle prick was nothing. She had faced far more pain. Her endurance level – no one could match.

"Did you feel the pinch? Pearce asked. He noticed that Ria was lost in her thoughts and looking at her brothers instead. There was a different spark in her eyes. She was thinking about something.

Kamran thought, "I admire you, Ria. You are the most wonderful person I have ever met. At first, I was quite self-centered, but after knowing you I have changed my thoughts and I have started entrusting in you."

"Ria, what a lovely name and what an amazing person you are. Even though you are going through a lot of difficulties, yet you are always smiling and never hesitate to lend an arm to your dear ones.", Pearce thought.

Both the friends shared a telepathic moment. Life was like a storybook for all of them. There was suspense, intrigue, love, friendships, adventure. There was never a dull moment in their life. There was a moral on every page, and the best part of this tale was that the love, bonding, and camaraderie between brothers, sister, and friends was strong. Nothing was going to break that.

"What is with that glare, Ria? "Nathaniel asked.

"Okay, all done. Sis, can you please try moving now. But tell all of us one thing, why were you giving us that glare?" Raymond asked.

"It was not a glare. I was just looking at you and thinking how concerned you all were for me, the way Ray injected the needle in me so that I don't feel anything, the way Kamran and Pearce were telepathing and that Nath was holding me so that I stay like a stiff rock, and not move,"

Kamran and Pearce were speechless. Ria was amazing. At this moment, they felt they were more like brothers than friends!

***

As the boys got busy running tests on Ria's blood, our hero, Ria who was sitting on a chair heard a sudden whisper which got her off her place.

"I am here, Ria Walker; I followed your footsteps, and I smelled your flesh. Now, who can save you? You are weak and vulnerable…" The whisper trailed off.

"Nat, Ray." Did you all hear a strange, mysterious voice? Ria asked with a puzzled look on her face.

The boys were distracted as they were huddled over a table examining Ria's blood under a powerful microscope.

"Ria, what happened? What Voice?" Pearce said. He felt his heartbeat beating faster as he saw the puzzling look on Ria's face.

"Guys, I heard a whisper. Someone is coming for me. It was the same voice that spoke to me back at school. Ow! The numbness is back. I don't know if I can take it much longer," Ria whispered.

"Yeah, sis is correct. Even I can also sense a weird unknown presence of somebody. Who could it be? Guys, we must protect Ria. She won't be able to tackle the upcoming storm approaching us," Raymond said.

"I can!!!! Ow!" Ria screamed.

"Yeah, sure you can, and we might end up losing you "Permanently" this time. What do you have to say now?" Kamran retorted.

"Kamran, I know it is not worth taking the risk, but then I might sound like a coward now, but I guess we all must activate our camouflage mode on our Mactracks right now, this way even I will be safe and so will you all be. I will activate my scanning mode, and I will check for anything unusual," Ria said as she commanded her Mactrack.

"Ria, what a smart idea! This way all will be able to understand more about this problem of yours.", said Pearce as he patted Ria's shoulder.

"Everyone camouflage mode, now!" Nathaniel ordered.

***

A second later after everyone went to camouflage mode, a black creature came floating by. As soon as the creature entered the room which was completely silent, our heroes sensed an ill-smell of blood.

"What is with this ill-smell? It is unbearable. Oh god!" whispered Kamran, as he tried catching his breath.

"True, this smell is unbearable." Added Raymond.

The black creature floated around and scanned the entire room and spoke, "Ria Walker, I smell your presence, and the joy of murder runs through my veins, but, before I introduce you to your death, I shall offer you a last wish. Speak now."

Ria wondered, *"This... This awful creature. It smells like a hundred rotting corpses. It is asking me for my last wish. Why is this creature craving for my death so eagerly?"*

Raymond turned to the boys and whispered, "Who is this creature? Why is he/she craving for our sister's death? Is this creature living or non-living?"

"Don't talk brother, he/she might sense our presence," Nathaniel put a finger to his lips.

Ria sent a message telepathically to the boys, *"Everyone, listen to me, this voice, I have heard it somewhere."*

The boys looked at each other.

"Walker, I shall not address my prey with its first name as it is a sin. I can strongly smell your presence; your aura is powerful. I believe in superstition even though we are in a technology-driven era. I also sense the power in you, so why don't you join me, and together we can rule this world!" The creature let out an awful cackle as it spoke the last sentence.

Ria thought, *"Group, superstitions? Who is this person? Why do I sense as if he knows me, my secrets, my past, everything? I need to take the risk myself again, I must reveal my presence to know if this is the actual culprit or not?"*

This new development shook up the group. There was a creature who was hell-bent on hurting Ria, but they felt so helpless.

In her mind, Ria commanded for the camouflage mode to go off.

Once again, our hero took the risk. She knew what it was to fight for yourself, especially when it was the question of survival?

***

"Who are you? Why do I get the feeling that you are behind my numbness feeling? What do you want from me?" Ria said. She was now face-to-face with the shadowy figure cloaked in black.

"What a shame, the Ria Walker who was the smartest, is weak, vulnerable, and like a baby needing her brothers to take care of her. I guess this youngest Walker knows how to show her bravery this way, with her bodyguards surrounding her." The creature laughed out a raspy sound.

"I will show you, how dare you." Ria roared.

"Enough, I have no time to waste, and now, I must take your life without showing any mercy. You should be pleased that your death is written in my hands. @#&&##!!!!".

The creature chanted a spell, which neither Ria nor any of the other Tech Teens had heard before.

"Ah, I can't fight with this thing with powers… AH!!" Ria was on her knees, unable to move.

Nathaniel and the others rushed to Ria's aid.

"Back off, Mactrack petrification darts!!!" Nathaniel yelled.

"@#&&##!!!!" The creature screamed.

The creature disappeared in a wisp of black dust. All that remained was a mound of black dust beside Ria. It smelt like death. The Walker brothers were heartbroken to see their sister in so much pain.

"We told you not to be so stupid, then why, why do you always take the risk. Can you just listen for once? Imagine if anything would have happened to you then," Nathaniel said. He bent down to comfort Ria.

"I don't have words to say how sorry I am!" Ria could no longer sense the pain.

"What happened?" questioned Kamran

"I can no longer sense the pain!" Ria was back on her feet.

It was strange the pain suddenly vanished. Everyone knew something was fishy in this case. It was strange that in the creature's presence Ria's pain would increase but as soon as the creature departed the pain also did.

"What!? How can this be possible?" asked Pearce as he scratched his head.

"Anyways, whatever it maybe at least you are fine. That is what matters right now…" Raymond smiled nervously; he knew that troubles weren't over yet.

The situation was tense, none of them neither knew the cause of this numbness nor did they know why does the numbness pain increase in the creature's presences, and decrease with its departure?

***

It was around 6 pm, and the sun was setting and Ria knew that her mother would be worried sick, if she returned before they do so. So, Ria stood up, walked up to the boys and spoke to her brothers.

"Ray, Nat, let us head back home. Before mum, starts calling me or either of you two and yell that where the heck have, we been!?", Ria said as she was laughing hard.

"Agreed! Mom would surely call us up like more than a thousand times or even spam our phones with messages like 'Why haven't you three returned home!?'" Nathaniel giggled as he noticed everyone else also bursting out into laughter.

"Yeah, that is so true! But something else also is troubling me. Just before I fell on my knees, that creature directed a spell at me in a language which was hard to decipher.", replied Ria as she kept a smile on her face.

"What do you mean? He spoke in an unrecognizable language?" Kamran asked.

Ria nodded and said, "Yes, it seems so."

"Maybe this creature knows some ancient secret language for powerful spells" Pearce said.

"Yeah, but the scary part is that whatever that spell was, it surely wasn't used for a good purpose. Also, one more thing is for sure, whoever is behind all these attacks on me, he knows me and my powers too well." Said Ria as she picked up her backpack.

"Who do you think it is?" Raymond asked.

"I have no idea who it is? But whoever it maybe, we have no clue that how do they knows my strengths and weaknesses? Also, on that note, there is one more thing we have no idea what we are up against?" Ria said as she looked at the confused faces of the boys.

It was 6:15 by the time the chat between the teammates ended. Both the brothers called up their mom and asked if she was already home.

"Mom!? Are you already home!?" Raymond kept his phone on speaker and asked.

"Not yet, I am few miles away. I would be reaching home soon, and I better see you three! Or else no dinner for the three of you tonight!" It was Mariah on the other end and she did not sound so happy when her eldest son called up to ask that was, she home yet or not.

Raymond abruptly ended the call and everyone panicked especially the triplets who were rather more worried about dinner than the scolding. With that weird thought everyone yelled at Nathenial to teleport them back at home.

***

The triplets and their friends were at Nathenial's house. As Raymond turned back towards the stairs Mariah came in with two big plastic bags.

"Nat, Ria take these bags and keep it on the table. Oh! Hello Kamran, hello Pearce! How have you two been?" Mariah asked as she handed over the bags.

"We are doing great Mrs. Walker! How are you doing?" asked Pearce as he was fidgeting with his bag.

"I am doing fine! So, what brings you two here today?" Mariah questioned as she took off her shoes and kept them in the shoe rack.

"Oh, we all had to do some research on the history of America. So, we all were at the library and we just dropped by to say hi! And give Nat his journal back." Kamran spoke with a smile and opened his backpack taking out a blue journal and gave it to Nathenial.

The friends then bid goodbye and went to their homes. As soon as they left the Walkers freshened up and gathered at the dining area for dinner.

"So, how was your day kids?" asked Mariah.

"It was kind of boring as we had two lectures of history. And David our classmate fell asleep when we were learning about Quadratic sequences." Raymond laughed at the end.

"Hmm, this white sauce pasta is so good!" Ria said as she took a bite with delight.

"I knew that I would be late so I had bought dinner from outside!" Mariah smiled as she noticed her daughter enjoying the food.

Everything was normal, none of them remembered about the numbness. It was like a bad memory which had already vanished into thin air. And so, like that it was already bedtime. Everyone went to their room, and shut their eyes as they laid on their comfortable bed.

***

Ria tossed and turned in her sleep. She was dreaming and her dreams were dark and scary. She could hear moans and screams and a presence of an evil.

"Walker, I am back again to suck all your powers out. Ha! Who shall save you now? You will be slaughtered, right here right now," the creature said. Then it started that awful cackle again.

Suddenly Ria woke up.

"HUH! What a dream. It felt like that creature was here. Ah, the numbness is kind of killing me now. I guess, I have really terrible days ahead unless I can quickly find out who is behind all these mysterious attacks on me and dispose of the threat once and for all."

The windows in the room had been left open and the curtains were dancing in response to the howling wind outside. Ria walked to the window and looked outside. The crescent moon looked eerie tonight, the shape of a thin unhappy smile.

"You are right. Death awaits you, Walker. I shall show no mercy on you," the creature said. It was standing next to Ria.

Ria froze. She felt the presence of evil in her room. Her heart was skipping beats as she turned to her right to see the creature with its hollowed eyes staring back at Ria.

"AH!!!! The blood on its hands, that long thin knife ready to slaughter me.... Mum, Brothers!!!"

"Cry, beg, plead, but no one will come to rescue you for I have cursed everyone, death warriors listen to the great words, obey your master, and you shall be rewarded, fail me and death is certain," the creature screeched.

"Ah!!!! My, My numbness."

Ria's breathing slowed, her heartbeat was all but faint, her vision was blurring, and then a thin line of blood rolled down Ria's eye.

"MUM"

Her breath was cold as ice, and her body like a cold statue, lifeless and the pain running through the numbed veins.

"Mum, Mum, help! I cannot move, that black creature, brothers, brothers!!!"

Ria was calling out in pain and moans escaping from her mouth. It made it difficult for her to lay still on her bed.

"Ria, honey, wake up. It was a nightmare! Ria, you must hold yourself still, or else the pain will worsen. Oh no, her brothers are asleep. I must give her the tablets," Mariah said as she gasped for breath, but again ran down to her room.

***

Mariah came back with the bottle containing pink tablets and helped her moaning daughter to sit up, put one tablet in her mouth, she took the glass water which on the beside table in Ria's room, and held her daughter's neck allowing her daughter to drink the water.

"Mum, am I alive? Or is this a hallucination?"

"Sweetheart, you are alive, hold on, sit for a while. The medicine needs time to work. Until then, I shall get your brothers."

"Yeah, sure! But please come back quickly…" Ria said in a low but bold voice.

"Look, all the lights of your room are on. Nothing will happen. Just don't move from your bed."

Mariah ran to her son's room, keeping Ria's room door open, hoping she might call out if something happens.

"Boys, boys, get up! Nat, Ray, get up now," Mariah said loudly.

Nathaniel and Raymond shifted in their beds and slowly opened their eyes. They looked at Mariah and intuitively knew something was off. The brothers were both wide awake.

'Mum?' Nathaniel asked.

"Mum, what is it?" Raymond asked.

"Ria has just had a terrible nightmare. She saw the black creature, and she couldn't move in her dreams, and there was blood flowing down from her eyes. You two must sleep with her tonight. I do not want her to be alone."

Mariah had barely completed her sentence when a loud, piercing scream came from Ria's room. "Mum! Brothers!"

The three rushed to Ria's room, and there she was on the floor, moving backward with her shaking hands as she collided with the bathroom door.

"Back off, freak! Get away from our sister. Ray I shall now do my thing. Just ensure that the creature doesn't attack sis, mum, or you.", Nathaniel urged.

What a night. Evil was relentless. It refused to let go of Ria. Why was it after Ria?

"Now, you shall die freak. It is time to reveal who you are," Nathaniel said.

This felt like a repeat telecast of the events of the afternoon. Only this time, it was time to get rid of the evil.

"Maclets, Petrification darts," Nathaniel's voice boomed.

"@#$&&!!!" The creature spoke and disappeared.

It was weird for everyone especially the triplets, whenever Nathenial said Petrification Darts this creature would disappear. The brothers gently picked Ria and lay her on the bed.

"The creature's presence is negative; the medicine automatically stops working when this creature is present." Mariah said.

Ria, lied lifeless on her bed thinking, *"Where am I? What is this place? Hold on, I am not in my human form. I am a soul. This place is the inside of me, suffering, blood flowing paths have narrowed, and the medicine I just took is not showing any effect. Maybe I can give it a boost."*

Her soul had the potential to bring her back from dead, yet she needed to sustain herself with the help of this medicine and wipe out the poison from her blood.

"Oh no, I hope it is not too late. We cannot lose her now when we are so close to uncovering this mystery. Sis, please come back. I know it's not too late," Nathaniel was edgy as he held his sister's icy cold hands and sobbing. A drop of tears from Nathaniel's eyes fell on Ria's hands, bringing her back to her sense.

"Mum, Brothers. Huh! I am fine,"

"Ria, thank god, for a second, we thought we lost you," Mum shook her head.

"Ria, we shall free you from this misery soon. Tomorrow is the last day you will suffer from this poison. It will end tomorrow because I have found the culprit. We will catch it red-handed," Nathaniel smirked.

Mariah left the room and went back to her room. She knew she would have a troubled sleep tonight.

Raymond, kissed Ria's forehead and turned to get pillows from his room. But as he turned, he was stopped in his tracks as Ria had gripped his little finger.

"Nathaniel, I think Ria is not going to let go. I think she feels unsafe to be left alone even for a minute."

"Not to worry, I will be back with the pillows. Ria looks cute when she sleeps holding your little finger. It reminds me of those days when she was younger, and when she caught a cold. She would do this, hold on to one of our fingers," Nathaniel smiled.

Despite the temporary smiles, Mariah, Nathaniel, and Raymond knew that Ria was not out of danger. She had almost died tonight.

As Raymond waited for Nathaniel, he whispered, "Sis, this so unlike you, lying lifeless. Let us put an end to all this tomorrow."

Nathaniel opened the door slightly, seeing his elder brother playing with Ria's hair and not waking her up.

"Brother, she was in so much agony at school, in the robot, and now at home – what a draining day for her. At least I am at peace that she is finally sleeping. But I also fear that she is frightened of that creature for some reason which we don't know," Nathaniel said.

"Yeah, now we both need some sleep. Let us cuddle up to her and make her feel warm. Let her feel safe and protected tonight."

Ria turned to Nathaniel's side and stretched her arms out. He cuddled her and smiled.

***

"Mum"

"Yes, what is it boys?"

With such noisy brothers, there was no need for an alarm to wake Ria up.

"Where is Ria?" They both asked.

"She is at the table, waiting for both of you. Better be quick before she finishes your breakfast too,"

"Mum, you look lovely today?" Ria complimented Mariah.

“Thank you, honey! You look good too. I like your fashion sense, a combination of a girl and boy. Your taste in fashion is impeccable!”

“Thanks, mum. I can already smell the amazing aroma of the pancakes. Please make them quickly!” Ria said as she finished drinking her glass of warm water.

While the breakfast was getting ready the brothers got ready and came down to eat their breakfast and start their regular routine. But today was something special, it was Thursday and everyone knew that they had two lectures of sports.

***

At the table everyone sat and started eating making a lot of noises and that is when Raymond spoke.

“I might eat more today. As we have two lectures of sports.” Giggled Raymond.

The doorbell rang at that very moment and Nathenial got up to open the door. Kamran and Pearce were at the door. Before Nathenial could say anything, they pushed him aside and ran straight to the breakfast table as if they already knew that they may miss something significant if they were even a minute late. Nathenial stood there at the door with his mouth wide open with amusement though this was not something new at all. Every Thursday Mariah cooked Pancakes for breakfast which all the children loved. It was a routine for Kamran and Pearce to drop in every Thursday before going to school to enjoy their favorite Pancakes. Mariah on the other hand enjoyed making the Pancakes for her children and their friends.

“Mrs. Walker, can I have some more pancakes please,” Pearce inquired while hastily finishing up the last pancake left on his plate. Mariah smiled and handed over few pancakes to Kamran and Pearce.

“Duh, brother! Hand me over the Maple syrup bottle!” Raymond said to Nathenial as he was getting eager to snatch the bottle.

Soon all of them were having a nice time enjoying the Pancakes and narrating merrily about some of the amusing events that had occurred in their school. The room was filled with laughter and joy and for a moment the Tech Teens had forgotten all the ordeal they had gone through and what was about to come.

Suddenly, Nathenial noticed that his watch was beeping. It was a low frequency beep that only Nathenial could hear. There was a coded message for him from Xandacross, “Come soon…Anomaly detected in Ria’s blood”. The message sent a cold shiver down his spine. He immediately got up from the breakfast table. There was a panic written all over his face. Although he tried to hide it so as to not alarm Mariah, but it was so evident that Mariah immediately noticed it.

“What is it Nathenial? Why are you so alarmed all off a sudden as if something has bitten you? Mariah asked worriedly.

“Oh nothing, I… Nat blanked. He was caught off guard and was not sure what to tell his Mom. His mind was racing to figure out how to come out of the situation without alarming her.

Raymond immediately sensed that Nathenial was trying to hide something from Mariah. Whatever it was, it must have something to do with Ria and her recent numbness problem because that was the only thing that could bring such concerning looks on Nathenial's face. Raymond immediately jumped in the conversation to help Nathaniel from the awkward situation.

***

"Mom, don't worry about it. I just remembered that Nathenial had told me yesterday that he had to finish a school project and submit it today. He had asked my help for it. It somehow slipped from my mind too. I am sure Nat just remembered about his pending project work. If he does not finish it today than Mr. Xavier, our science teacher will be surely upset".

"Nat, let's go into your study room and quickly finish your project work. We both can work on it while the others can continue with their breakfast. I am anyway done eating three Pancakes so I am full", Raymond signaled something to Nathenial from the corner of his eyes.

Ria, Kamran and Pearce knew something was amiss but pretended as if they were unaware of anything and continued enjoying the Pancakes. They knew it was best to continue eating and keep Mariah busy with them giving Ray and Nat some time to take care off whatever issue had surfaced up. They trusted Ray and Nat to signal to them if they needed their help.

***

Ray and Nat immediately got up from the breakfast table and proceeded towards their study room without saying a single word.

"What's the matter Nat? what is suddenly bothering you? I can tell from your face that whatever it is, can't be good news", Raymond probed Nathenial.

"You are right, Ray. I just got a very cryptic message from Xandacross". Nat then showed the coded message that he had received on his watch from Xandacross.

"This is really not good news. Let us go right now to Xandacross and see what this is all about", We do need to return back as soon as possible otherwise if Mom finds that we are missing from our study room then she will be alarmed and may force us to share our secrets" Ray remarked.

***

A few minutes later both brothers were in the control room of Xandacross. Nathenial had teleported them directly from their study room.

Both were staring at a huge screen in front of them which had details of Ria's blood test. Everything looked normal except the indication of some anomaly which was pointing towards presence of some strange poison in Ria's blood. The toxicology report was unable to trace the source of the poison. It checked against all known metals and chemicals that could cause poisoning, but none matched the traces found in Ria's blood. It was because of this poison that Ria was having occasional numbness in her legs followed by shaking and fainting. Unfortunately, the high-tech scanner in Xandacross was unable to recommend cause or treatment for the poison in Ria's blood

Luckily, the poison was in a very minute amount and was not affecting any of Ria's living tissues, at least not yet. Raymond and Nathaniel were baffled to see Poison in Ria's blood.

The two brothers spent next 30 minutes at Xandacross pondering about their next moves and whether, or not to disclose their latest finding about Ria's numbness issue to Ria, Mariah and their friends. They decided that it was best to tell Ria as well as the others and in fact they could probably ask their mother if she had any idea how Ria may have got poison in her blood.

Nathaniel and Raymond transported themselves back to their study room once again.

***

Back at their home, Ria, Kamran and Pearce had already finished their breakfast. They came to the study room hoping to see Nat and Raymond there but were surprised to see the room empty.

Ria connected with Raymond and Nathaniel telepathically and realized that her brothers were at Xandacross and were returning home.

A few minutes later, Ray and Nat appeared in their study room and found Ria, Pearce and Kamran waiting impatiently for them.

"What did you find out Ray and Nat? am I dying?" Ria asked, trying to hide her fears.

"Well Ria, we found out what is causing your numbness however, unfortunately we are far from figuring out a treatment for it.", Nathaniel said looking as if he had solved a mysterious case.

"So. what is it? Now tell us quickly and do not deepen the mystery further and raise our curiosity", Pearce said impatiently.

"It looks like Ria has traces of some mysterious poison in her blood which is causing her numbness issue".

"Poison in blood? What on earth that is supposed to mean Nat? Where would poison come from in Ria's blood? This is got to be a mistake" Kamran said confidently.

"No, we checked the report prepared by the hi-tech scanner at Xandacross very carefully. There is no room for any mistake here", Raymond remarked.

"so, what do we do now? Should we ask Mom if she has any clue how I may have got traces of poison in my blood? Ria asked.

"No, we should avoid getting Mom involved in it. She will panic and be worried more knowing about the poison in your blood", Nathaniel said.

"For now, we don't need to worry about the poison too much because it is not life threatening as it is present in small amount in Ria's blood. We will eventually find a way to remove it from her blood", Raymond said.

"True, but we need to find out why I have the numbness in my feet, whenever the creature attacks me. It is, as if the creature manipulates the poison in my blood to momentarily paralyze my limbs and drain out all my energy. I feel terribly week during and right after the creature's attack", Ria reminded everyone.

"Yes, we need to soon find out how the creature uses Ria's poison in her blood against her, before things get out of hand terribly and Ria's gets hurt.", Kamran jumped into the conversations.

"I think all off this can wait for some time. We need to first head towards school. We are already late for our science lecture, Mr. Xavier, will be terribly upset if we are even 5 minutes late and won't let us attend the lecture", Pearce reasoned.

Half an hour later, our Tech Teen team were in the school attending Mr. Xavier's special lecture, "Poison, their sources and cure", was it a mere coincidence, or something sinister was at play here?

After Ms. Xavier's lecture was over, Nathaniel, Ria, Raymond and the others decided to go to the school cafeteria for some light snacks. As they were walking towards the cafeteria, they heard someone yelling at them from behind.

"Raymond, how dare you wear that jacket? You better remove it right now," Jacky said. He was incensed.

Jacky was angry because Raymond was wearing the exact jacket that Jacky was wearing.

"You don't order me around, buddy. You are a jerk, and if you are forgetting, I am not one of your spineless friends who would listen to you shouting orders at them."

"I guess then you might listen to your sister, Puny Walker."

Ria who was standing a minute ago was now on her knees.

"Hey, let me get some help for you." Jacky gave a worried look and whistled.

Ria was puzzled. When did he turn nice? Who was he going to seek help from?

"Ouch! Oh no, I feel the numbness creeping back. Guys, do you think we will be ever able to catch the culprit behind these attacks on me," Ria asked.

Just then, the black creature came and circled around the Tech Teens as he floated.

"What a pity, no matter how much I try, you always slip out of my grasp Ria Walker. I am going to kill you for sure sooner or later, and if you think that you can defeat me…you are dead wrong."

"HUH, try your luck, beast."

"@#$%!!!!" the creature chanted the spell.

Nothing happened.

"Wait, what, how on earth is this possible? How could you escape my attack?" The creature was floating feverishly.

"Flabbergasting right, I knew that you would chant your spell and make me weak, but wait, let's not spoil the suspense. You will know what I did in the end when I finally destroy you!"

"Wow! I should have never underestimated her. She is way stronger than I thought, but she is also naïve. She thinks she can win, but she is dead wrong, I am the Master of Poison attacks and no one can withstand my numbness attacks for long," the creature thought to himself.

"What happened, creature? No more sly attacks to render Ria powerless. My sis has finally figured out a way to counter your attacks. I guess you should realize that now it is best for you to surrender when you have the chance to do so," Nathaniel smirked.

"Go on, try your luck! We won't be soft on you," Pearce added.

The boys and Ria had blown the conch shell of war. It was game time. With two protective brothers, a half-injured soldier, an intelligent warrior, and a funny, but cunning fox, the creature was in trouble.

"Ria, don't worry, this fight will be over soon, just hang-in there", Nathaniel cries out to Ria to boost her confidence.

As Nathaniel cries out, something suddenly flashes before his eyes. It was as if he had a premonition of something that was going to happen, except that it was much more vivid, as if he had travelled to a future time for a second. He saw that Ria was gasping for her breath. The creature had rendered Ria powerless with one of his powerful attacks. She was lying completely motionless on the floor as if there was no life in her body. Nathaniel panicked seeing this and wanted to shout to others for help, but he felt as if he was choking and was not able to utter anything. Then suddenly everything just vanished, and Nathaniel was back in the present. It just happened so fast that Nathaniel did not even had the time to think of what had just happened. He suddenly heard the creature challenging Ria.

"Okay, I want to take on Ria one on one, you all can take on my minions. I think you will be worthy just of that," the creature laughed manically.

"Take this you monster, you have no right to live this life. Now when you had the chance why didn't you take the opportunity to wipe it off you?" Ria glared at the creature as she extended her fist towards the creature.

Ria's fist was stopped by the creature's attack. He placed his finger on her forehead and started chanting a longer spell compared to the other times.

"Ria, back off quickly. Do not go closer to the creature", Nathaniel tried to warn Ria. But it was too late.

"AH! My, My heart… You monster." Ria cried with pain.

"Guys!!!! Ria, has been attacked. Her life is in danger," Nathaniel screamed.

The next hour was like a nightmare in the daytime. A force had immobilized the boys. They could not move. They watched in horror as the color slowly drained from Ria's face, then her body. Nathaniel's worst fear had come true.

"Back off, everyone! I can still fight and send this creature to hell," Ria spoke valiantly even though she was gasping for her breath. Her heart was beating fast. And then before anyone can do anything, Ria collapsed on the floor lifeless.

Nathaniel realized that this is exactly he had witnessed magically just few minutes back. So, it was not a dream. It was actual future event that Nathaniel had witnessed. He was thrown into a future and then magically taken back to present by some unknown powerful force. However, even knowing the tragic future, it seems he was unable to stop it from happening. Ria was meeting her tragic fate. She was on the verge of dying and there was noting he could do.

Ria lied motionless on the floor. Her heart had stopped, so it seems. A tsunami of emotions broke out as the boys watched the slow painful death of their sister and friend.

"Petrification darts! You monster, why are you doing this to Ria? What harm she has done to you? Why don't you take my life instead?" Nathaniel screamed.

The creature laughed hysterically.

"HA! HA! HA! you are so naïve like your dying sister. Why do think I would like to know; a bunch of teenagers like you? I just want your sister!" said the creature as he saw Nathenial shaking a bit.

"Who are you? What do you want from my family? Why have you targeted my sister?"

"Huh! Look, who is asking me questions. You are in no position to ask me questions. I can just end it here!" roared the creature as he pointed towards Ria.

Raymond dropped to his knees and cradled Ria in his arms.

"Ria, please don't leave us." Pearce cried out in frustration.

"Come on Ria, please don't leave us." Kamran could not complete his sentence as he too burst into tears.

"No not again, how can this happen? How can life be so tough on us" Raymond sobbed.

"You jerk, what do you want from my family?" Nathaniel asked the creature.

"I don't want anything from you or your family. I just want the power to rule over the world and nothing else. You fools are unaware that Ria has been given deadly powers. Powers that are beyond imagination. Powers that are so destructive that it can wipe out our earth from the universe and destroy our entire solar system. The same power can recreate another wonderful world. So, you see I just want to drain out all her powers from her soul and

make them part of my powers. By the time I drain all her powers from her soul, she will be dead." grinned the creature.

"Nathaniel!!!" Jacky screamed.

"What happened Jacky?" Nathanial said in frustration.

"Nat, we need to do something. Ria is still lying lifeless," Raymond moaned.

Jacky shook his head. The poor Walkers. He then took out a purple bottle from his pocket and handed it over to Nathaniel.

"Take this antidote. It will temporarily block all the effects of the poison which is present in Ria's blood that this creature is manipulating. Go and save your sister!"

"But...how.... did you know..." Nathaniel spluttered in disbelief.

Jacky did not reply. He just shook his head.

"It is going to be alright Ria, let the medicine slide down your throat and let it work as Jacky says.

A sudden moan escaped from Ria's mouth.

"Thank lord, she is breathing again. Ria is fine," Pearce said. He was now clapping his hands.

"Thank God, it is finally over! But Jacky, why hasn't Ria opened her eyes yet?" Both the brothers spoke almost at the same time.

"The medicine has just started to show its magic, she will regain her sense back in an hour or so." Jacky smiled at his juniors.

"I shall not spare that monster!" barked Raymond.

As all the boys focused their attention back on the creature, they noticed that the creature was nowhere to be seen. He had already fled from the scene and they let out a sigh of relief to see their sister well.

Chapter 55 – A Normal Life

The Poison Problem Ended and the Heroes where Ready to Embark on a Fun and Adventurous Trip Visiting an Old Relative…

25th October…

The day was Sunday, and the triplets were enjoying their three months' vacation, about 25 days had already passed, and everyone was enjoying the last days of the warm sun until the chilly winter came to visit.

***

"Oh, my goodness, for heaven's sake brother, don't mess up the test model of the robot which I took almost 2 weeks to make!," Ria yelled at Nathaniel who had decided to annoy Ria, yet again.

"Honestly guys, do you mind keeping your voices low for the time being? I am unable to solve this math equation with all this commotion." Raymond was frustrated with his younger siblings.

While the triplets continued their little squabble, their mother Mariah came running from the kitchen to answer the phone that was lying on the table.

***

Mariah pulled out a chair and sat, placing one hand on the table and the other holding the phone with her left ear.

"Hello? Who is this?" questioned Mariah.

"Hmm, I guess you don't recognise the voice of your little sister, do you Mariah?" a soft toned voice replied.

"Oh my god! Casandra, my little sister, how have you been? It's been ages since we have spoken. How are you?," asked Mariah.

"I am well, and how have you been doing these days? Also, I have something exciting to share with you. I am finally getting married!"

Mariah was delighted to hear the news which she had been longing to hear for many months. Mariah got married before Casandra but due to her job Casandra had to move to Seoul in South Korea.

"Wow, I am so happy for you sis! But tell me one thing, whom are you getting married to? What does he do?," Mariah was bombarding her little sister with questions.

"His name is Ahn Leo, and he was born in South Korea, but he studied in America. He is a doctor and has his own hospital in Bay City. So, we will permanently move to Bay City."

"That's amazing! Hey, I have an idea, how about the kids and I come to South Korea to pay you a visit? The kids are getting bored anyway. Ria's favorite boy band The Royal Rockers, will be performing in Seoul in two weeks. I had promised her that I would take her to their concert."

Mariah was planning a surprise vacation for her kids.

Mariah's conversation lasted for almost an hour; she didn't realize that her kids were calling for her. She ended the call and immediately went to the living room to see what the commotion was about.

***

"What happened? Why are you guys calling me?" questioned Mariah.

"Mum, we all are hungry. We need food, cause if we don't, we might go wild and break a few showpieces," the triplets all spoke together.

Mariah chuckled, as the 7-year-old side of her kids still lived within them.

Mariah thought, "*Their smiling faces are amazing but I cannot erase the pain that my daughter has suffered through in recent times.*"

Ria noticed her mother was lost in her own thoughts so she snapped her out of it and brought her back to reality.

"Mum, Mum!" roared Ria.

"Huh? What happened honey?" Mariah was a bit startled.

"Mum, where are you lost? Can you please serve us lunch quickly? I am dying of hunger…" Ria made her baby face.

***

"Ria, honey come here please! I need your help!" called out Mariah

"Coming mum! You both will be in trouble later, remember that brothers!," Ria stuck her tongue out at the end of the last word.

"Mummy, why did you call me?" questioned Ria

"Honey, take these plates and go and set them on the table. Also, I have kept the spoons and forks on top of one plate so please set those as well," said Mariah.

Mariah handed the cutlery to her daughter, and Ria went to the dining table and set them up nicely and came back to take the glasses to complete the set up.

"Brothers, lunchtime!" Ria commanded.

Both the brothers raced up to the table, but Nathenial collided with Ria and she fell along with a chair hard on the ground.

"Ow! That hurt….," Ria groaned a little rubbing her head.

Nathenial and Raymond both were a little startled but they both helped Ria up and Raymond picked up the chair and returned it to its spot.

"Are you okay sis? I hope you didn't get hurt?" Nathenial asked with concern.

"Yup, I am fine. I didn't get hurt," Ria replied with a smile.

"Am I invisible? Or did I make myself invisible, that you couldn't see me brother?" Ria giggled.

"Nice sense of humor sis!" said Raymond as he burst out laughing.

***

"Okay, what do you guys want to eat first?" asked Mariah

The triplets were clueless about what was cooked for lunch, they only knew that their mother was cooking a special lunch to celebrate the start of the school holidays.

Mariah opened the lids of the serving bowls one by one and the triplets were shocked to see their favorites.

"Ramen and steak!" exclaimed the triplets.

Ramen and steak was one of the most favorite dishes of the triplets.

"Mum, can I ask you something?" asked Nathenial.

"Yes, honey anything...,"Mariah replied in a low tired voice.

"Whom were you talking to when we were creating a ruckus?" Nathenial kind of seemed suspicious.

"Oh, it was a very old friend of mine. We haven't talked in years. She has invited us to visit her, so I thought we could visit her. What do you guys think?" asked Mariah.

Mariah knew that even though Nathenial didn't hear the entire conversation he suspected his mother. How long would Mariah be able to keep this secret?

"Hmm, not a bad thought mum, after all we have three months of vacations, we will become lazy heads staying home all day. Also, we have already explored the entire Bay City, probably visiting a new place would be amazing!" Ria sounded excited about the trip.

But little did Ria know that her mother was planning something very special for her. Yet, even within the fun atmosphere, there was something which bothered Ria, but she kept it hidden in the very deepest corner of her heart.

"Agreed with sis, I am also ready for this trip!," exclaimed Raymond. He was also pretty pumped up for this trip.

"Sign me up as well! But where are we going? When are we going?," Nathenial was all ready as well.

"It's all a surprise, but for now, all I can tell you is that we will be leaving this Sunday."

After lunch, the siblings decided to do their own thing. After dinner, the triplets headed to the terrace – their favourite spot. That evening, Ria had arrived earlier and was patiently waiting for the arrival of her brothers.

Ria was lying down with her eyes shut, earphones on listening to something, and hand placed behind her head. She was relaxed and was peacefully enjoying the breeze which played with her hair.

"BOO!," shouted Nathenial, jolting Ria.

"Lord, you guys scared me to death."

Ria removed her earphones and kept them in her pocket. She sat up folding her legs, and looked up at the stars lost in her thoughts?

"So, what are you thinking?," asked Raymond.

"Oh, I was just thinking about the trip, where is mum taking us?" asked Ria.

Raymond quickly added, " In my opinion it's better not to think about the place and focus on getting ready for this trip."

***

It was finally Sunday, the day of the trip. Even though the triplets were excited, their mother was even more excited to watch their reactions upon discovering the secret.

"Kids, are you all ready? We have to leave within ten minutes as our cab is on its way, we don't want to miss our flight!" exclaimed Mariah with a tone of excitement as she spoke every word.

"Ouch! This stupid door, I am sure it has some problems with me," Nathaniel spoke. Mariah knew that once again, Nathenial had bumped into the bathroom door.

"Son, I hope you know that blaming the door won't work, it still will be there for the rest of your life," Mariah said.

"Mum, I am ready. Woah, are there rocks or clothes in my suitcase? Mummy, can you help me bring down the suitcase please?" Ria was flustered as she dragged her suitcase to the edge of the stairs.

Mariah went upstairs and aided her daughter to bring her suitcase down. In the meantime, the boys were still squabbling about not being able to find something or the other.

"Okay, we are also ready mum. But now will you please tell us where you are taking us?" asked the boys as their voice overlapped.

"Boys, please hurry up. Come down quickly, we are getting late!" said Mariah still trying to hold on to the surprise.

A loud beep startled Ria and she realised the cab had arrived.

"Everyone, hurry up, the cab has arrived, Nath, Ray come down!," There was clear excitement in Ria's voice.

***

Everyone was pumped up for the vacation after what they had been through. They deserved a proper family vacation, to get a chance to get close to each other once again.

"Oh lord, you slowpokes move it," said Ria as she finished tying her shoelaces.

Both the brothers ran down those stairs bumping and crashing into each other, and at last; falling on top of each other.

"Woah, get off me you heavy mountain! Ugh, did my skull crack?," Nathenial pushing his brother off his back who was struggling after falling.

"Stop laughing like a monkey and help us up!" the brothers roared at their sister.

"Come on, hurry you three, we have to reach the airport on time.," Mariah couldn't wait anymore.

The atmosphere had a certain calm after all the chaos. The boys dragged their luggage down the last two stairs and into the living room, where they kept it near the couch arm rest and went on to put on their shoes.

"We are all set to go!," announced the brothers.

***

This trip was special. The Walkers led busy lives and that did not leave much time for fun activities. And let's not forget the triplets, saving the world.

Putting the daily grind aside, the day had come to forget that for a moment and setting off on an adventure to a new place.

***

Once all the luggage was placed in the cab, the ride to the airport was relatively smooth and they arrived there in 30 minutes.

***

The line was quite short for the bag-drop, and the family were served at the counter within five minutes. At the bag-drop counter, Mariah was completing all the formalities, while Ria was staring at the airline name plate, trying to guess where they would be flying to.

"Hmm, SK airlines? Pretty short and simple, but what's the full form?," Ria asked Nathenial.

Nathaniel just shook his head.

Nathenial and Ria were holding hands, waiting for their mother to complete the formalities so that they could continue on to the security check-in. After fifteen minutes or so, the boarding passes were safely tucked away in the passport as Mariah smiled.

While heading towards the security check area, Mariah questioned the triplets if they had a clue about where they were going?

All three just looked at her and shook their heads in unison.

Mariah thought it was time to reveal to her children where they were headed.

"We are going to meet your Aunt."

The triplets looked at Mariah quizzable expression. There were expecting Mariah to share more, but her stiff silence was a sign that more would be shared with them when Mariah was ready.

***

There was a very long wait at security. Some travelers were not following instructions and this led to their backs being placed through the X-ray machine again.

Finally, the Walkers cleared security and made their way towards the boarding gate.

"Ugh, do we have to wait again?," Ria sighed as there was a line at the boarding gate too!

"We are going to South Korea?" squealed Ria. South Korea.

Finally, the secret was out. The monitor above the boarding gate displayed the flight number and the destination.

The brothers high-fived each other. The family hugged each other. The kids had lots of questions but Mariah put a finger to her lips and told the children that she would answer all their questions while they waited in the lounge area.

***

Half an hour had when a tall man wearing the airline uniform picked up a mic and made an announcement.

"Dear passengers, we are extremely sorry but the flight has been delayed by 15 minutes due to bad weather and traffic on the runway due to which arriving flight are unable to land. We shall begin with the boarding as soon as the weather clears up." Said the man over the mic.

The look on everyone's face waiting there explained their frustration, but what else could they do except waiting there patiently for the traffic to clear out the weather to be good.

***

The boarding room was growing restless.

"Ugh, waiting is so frustrating.," said Ria as she looked at her watch.

"What else can we do other than waiting? Don't worry the boarding will begin soon enough.," said Raymond as he took his phone and headphones.

Suddenly, Ria stood up grabbing her backpack and began walking, but stopped as her mother called out.

"Honey, where are you going?," questioned Mariah.

"Oh, I will be back in five minutes. Don't worry I will be nearby. If boarding begins, ring me on my phone.," said Ria as she walked away disappearing in the crowd.

***

Ria walked into a fancy coffee shop. She wanted a Frappuccino. Riya did not intend to dose off on the plane so quickly.

"Ria, here you go, your Strawberry Frappuccino.," said the barista with a smile on her face.

Ria smiled back saying thank you and walked towards the boarding gate.

***

"Ah, finally she's here.," thought Mariah.

Ria saw how anxious her mother looked and increased her speed

"So, you went to buy yourself a Frappuccino huh?,"

"Yeah…," Ria knew her mother didn't seem so happy about her buying the Frappuccino.

"Should I throw it? You didn't seem too pleased about…," she continued with the same tone.

"No dear, I am surprised you are drinking a sweet-laden drink considering you are on that new diet."

"It's my cheat day," Ria winked at her mother.

"Ugh, how much longer do we have to wait?," asked Nathenial taking off his headphone.

"I hope they start with boarding soon.," said Ria.

Ria decided to walk up to the counter to ask when they would be flying.

***

Ria walked over to the counter and asked about the situation. The customer service agent replied that there was no update and as soon as they had some information, they would make an announcement.

***

Ria walked back to her mother and brothers and she sat beside Raymond who was listening to music.

"Ray, hey Ray. Wake up.," said Ria shaking Raymond holding his arm.

Raymond was sleeping peacefully and didn't even move a bit, so Ria slowly moved close to his ear and removed his headphone.

"Huh?," Raymond woke up rubbing his eyes.

"Have we started boarding?," he had no idea what he was saying.

"No, but let's play cards," Ria replied with frustration in her voice.

"Passengers of flight SK 895, flying to South Korea, please get ready for the boarding.,"

The triplets were discussing about the things they would do when they arrive in South Korea.

As their tickets were scanned, there was electricity of excitement running in the air.

"Oh my god, why do I feel this sudden current of happiness running inside me?," asked Nathenial.

It was not only Nathenial who felt that current but the entire Walker family who felt it too as they walked through the airbridge towards the plane.

***

As the entire family entered the plane, they felt more alive than they had felt in a very long time. They felt as if the world were reincarnated for them to live freely without fear.

"Which one is our seat?," questioned Ria after passing two seat rows.

"This one.," pointed Mariah.

"Mum, you got to be kidding? This, this can't be our seat!," the triplets did get louder at the end.

"Yes, it is!," Mariah exclaimed.

It was probably hard for the triplets to digest that they were travelling in business class.

Nathenial took the window seat, Ria the middle, and Raymond, the isle. Mariah sat on the aisle seat next to Raymond..

"This is so embarrassing. I am almost fifteen and I am afraid to fly," Riya whispered.

***

All the passengers going to South Korea had boarded, and now the air hostesses began demonstrating the safety instructions to the passengers, while our youngest hero grabbed her brother's arms quietly without even them noticing and shut her eyes tightly as the aircraft began moving towards the runway.

"Huh?," said the brothers as they felt someone holding their arms.

As the brothers turn around; they see Ria, with her eyes closed and muttering something to herself.

"I guess that this fear will remain with Ria," giggled Nathenial as Raymond and him both placed their hands on top of Ria's hand.

The plane slowly turned and positioned itself on the runway for takeoff.

"Okay, wait what the…," as soon as Ria let go of her brother's arms; she saw both of them snoring.

"Ugh, seriously, they fell asleep before the flight was not even in the air! Annoying brothers…," Ria pouted and put on her headphones and played music. With her eyes shut, she slowly drifted into the melodies of the song.

***

After a while, the brothers were awake and noticed Ria with her eyes shut.

"Is she really sleeping? Or acting to sleep?" wondered Raymond.

As the brothers turn around and sat straight facing the screen in front of them, they didn't realize that Ria sat up.

"Nathenial and Raymond...," Ria grabbed her brother's shirt collar from behind like a ghost.

"WOAH!!" the brother's turned to see their sister like an angry woman this time.

This is our hero's specialty that one moment she has a certain look on her face and the next moment she changes it according to the situation.

"Sis, what do you think the cuisine in South Korea is like?" a random question but one of Ria's interests was asked by Nathenial.

***

"Dear passengers, we have already started with the descend, we will be landing shortly," announced the pilot over the mic.

"I didn't even realize that we have started with our descend," said Nathenial as he stretched his stiff joints.

Raymond and Ria were busy watching a movie, while Mariah was reading a book, and Nathenial, was just staring out of the window at clouds.

A sudden thought popped up in Nathenial's mind as he silently watched the clouds as the plane continued to descend, *"It's so peaceful, seeing everyone looking forward to this trip, and obviously why won't they? After all our lives have been through a roller coaster filled with adventures and problems. For the family to come together like this is indeed a blessing."*

"Finally, the movie is over," said Ria as she removed her earphones and stretched.

"It's beautiful, isn't it brother?"

"Oh yes, it is not only beautiful but also peaceful. Which movie were you watching with such interest?" Nathenial was calm and relaxed.

"It is a suspenseful mystery where a detective is trying to solve a mystery where he is actually the main culprit," Ria said with a smile on her face.

"How interesting. The detective is the antagonist," Nathenial scrunched his face. He was not a fan of mystery and suspense.

"The plot was very interesting. It kept me guessing till the end. I had a narrowed down the suspects to two people, but I was so wrong."

"Ugh, my ears they are hurting," on the other hand Raymond was complaining of the sharp pain in both his ears due to change in air pressure.

Ria's eyes narrowed and she uttered a triggering statement, "You have low tolerance to pain brother."

Raymond was triggered and would have attacked Ria like a pack of crazy hungry wolves at this instant, but he didn't want to create a scene; so, he let her remark slide.

Ten minutes later, the city was finally in sight, but the view was hidden again by dark clouds as the aircraft continued its final descend.

"Wow, what a beautiful chemistry it is. Probably, the rain also adores travelling," said Raymond.

A few passengers nearby started laughing. Raymond did not realise how loud he could be at times.

***

At last, the plane landed at Incheon International Airport. The excitement dose hit with twice the strength as compared to when they boarded the plane for South Korea.

Raymond relaxed his stiff joints and so did other passengers. They felt like old people. Keeping the jokes aside, the hearts of all the tourists in that plane raced as fast as a jaguar.

Ria tapped on Raymond's shoulder as he leaned towards her and she spoke, "Even though we have traveled before, but why does this feel like the first time on a family vacation?"

Raymond just smiled. He wanted to enjoy this moment.

***

As the aircraft came to halt in front of an airbridge, and the engine was shut off. There was a two second silence until the passengers unbuckled their seat belts. The airbridge was attached to the door and the aircraft doors finally opened.

The airhostess took over the mic and announced, "Dear passengers, we have arrived at Incheon international airport; the temperature outside is 25."

Raymond stood up and opened up the overhead compartment and took out his laptop bag and kept it on his seat.

The airhostess once again announced, "Dear passengers, your checked-in luggage will be at arrival on belt number three."

***

Mariah stood up seeing the line ahead of her move; and so; did the triplets. The brothers said goodbye to the airhostess, but Ria bowed to the airhostess and the airhostess did the same thing. The brothers felt that was an awkward gesture.

"Why did you bow looking at the airhostess?," questioned Nathenial.

"Oh, you didn't know? Koreans often bow for many things like; thank you, hello, goodbye, I am sorry," Ria bowed as she chuckled.

***

As the family walked out of the airbridge and entered the airport terminal, the boys headed towards the washroom while Mariah asked Ria something as her patiently waited for Nathenial and Raymond.

"Honey, how do you know that Koreans bow when they say goodbye and other things which you said back there? We have never mentioned this at home. So how?" Mariah was curious.

"Mum, when we have free lectures at school; I often sit in the Korean class and listen to th teacher talk about South Korea and its culture. Though, I want to ask would you mind if I dropped Dutch at school and took an Asian language?" Ria had a certain attraction towards Asians.

"Why not. I believe you should study what you want to. Gone are the days where you choose to study what your parents want you to study," winked Mariah.

***

The brothers walked out together and saw the mother and daughter in conversation and decided that they had to interrupted it, even though they knew that their mother would not be too pleased.

"So, what is the conversation about? Mind, if we ask?," Raymond had a certain sweet way of interrupting a conversation.

"Your sister says that she wants to drop Dutch as a language and take up an Asian language at school. She asked if I had any objection, and I really don't have any objection," said Mariah

"Do you two have any problem with my taking the Asian languages at school?" asked Ria.

"I really don't have any objection," replied Nathenial.

"Nor do I," replied Raymond.

Ria smiled and the family headed towards the arrival hall to clear security and pick up their luggage. It was a good ten minute walk but the Walkers were excited!

***

"I will go get the trolley while, you guys can look out for the luggage," said Nathenial as he walked away to get the luggage trolley.

Nathenial returned in a minute with the trolley.

"That was quick bro!" said Raymond.

While waiting for their luggage, Ria saw a poster of her favorite band Royal Rockers; besides that; she noticed their wax dolls.

"Mum, can I go take a picture over there?"

Before Mariah could respond, Ria had run off towards the wax dolls.

***

Ria, first took a picture of the poster and then of all the wax dolls.

She started editing on her phone by adding the names of the group. There was the leader of the group Chin Seojun, the visual Kim Dae-seong, the main dancer Im Chan-yeol, and the main vocalist and Maknae Min Yae-joon.

While Ria continued editing on her phone, Nathenial and Raymond were collecting their luggage and turned back to notice that both their mother and sister weren't around.

Raymond looked around and spotted his mother at the duty-free shop, "Bro, mum is at the duty-free shop. Can you see sis?"

Nathenial knew exactly where Ria had sprinted off to.

***

"I knew it, I will always find Ria near a Royal Rockers poster. Such a fangirl she is ...," Nathaniel muttered.

***

As the Walker's were about to exit the arrival gate, the triplets noticed their mother was talking to someone.

"Hey! Have you reached, yet? We are waiting at arrival gate number 5," Mariah said to person.

A pale, tall, and thin woman with burgundy hair, was waving at them.

"Who is she, mum?" the siblings voices overlapped each other.

***

As the family approached the lady, Mariah hugged the lady, the triplets were shocked to hear what their mother said next.

"Hello sis! How have you been?" questioned Mariah.

Mariah turned back to see the triplets with their jaws dropped, and their faces blank with absolute confusion.

"I believe you guys have forgotten me?" the lady had kind eyes.

"No worries, I understand you guys haven't seen me in years. So, let me introduce myself. I am your aunt Casandra. I am sure when we last met you guys were maybe, 6 or 7.," continued Casandra.

Suddenly, the boys were taken to memory town.

"Aunt Casandra! It has been many years since we all last spoke," the boys exclaimed as they hugged their aunt and then let go of her.

While the boys spoke to their aunt, Ria was standing there dumbfounded. She was brought back to reality when her aunt walked up to speak to her.

"Hi, you are Ria, right?" asked Casandra

"Uhm, yes I am," Ria's voice was shaking not with fear but with shyness.

Casandra remembered her niece who was just two months old when she saw her, but today she is 15 years old.

"You have grown up so much, and you are so beautiful. Mariah has shared with me everything that has happened with you and the family, I am just glad you came back in one piece," Casandra smiled.

Ria finally lightened up with the smile. She knew that were more surprises in the store for her brothers and her.

***

"So, Ria what's the only thing you want to see or do here?" Casandra knew the obvious answer but wanted her niece to reply.

"Uhm, I want to go to the Royal Rockers concert."

This was the obvious answer that Casandra wanted to hear.

"Okay, who's your bias from Royal Rockers?" Casandra surely loved this Q & A.

"When I first began listening to them it was Im Chan-Yeol but now, my permanent bias is Min Yae-Joon," Ria replied beaming.

***

With this mini-Q&A session, the rest of the journey was silent, and no one spoke until they arrived in front of gigantic silver gate, where a young guard bowed and opened it.

"Wait, don't tell me that you own a mansion sis?" Mariah curiosity was the same as her daughter, just on difference; Mariah wasn't shy like her daughter.

Casandra had a creepy smile that answered Mariah's question.

***

The car stopped in front of a huge white patterned door, and the family stepped out with all sorts of looks on their face.

"Aunt, there is no way that this could be where you live!" Nathenial was speechless as his aunt nodded.

***

"Come on in," said Casandra leading the family into a gigantic royal living room filled with all sorts of paintings hanging on the wall and showpieces on the lonely corners of the living room.

"You have an impeccable taste in paintings aunt," said Ria examining every painting carefully as if she were to remake them.

"Miss. Casandra, the guest rooms are ready," a lady servant walked out from one of the rooms.

***

Everyone followed Casandra up the white stairs to the guest rooms. The triplets shared a room, while Mariah would share Casandra's room.

"Okay, I take the bed which is near to the window," said Ria running and then throwing herself on the bed.

Mariah and Casandra both chuckled and left the kids in the room. The silence didn't even last a second as Nathenial and Raymond argued as to who takes the bed near to the second window.

***

"Oh Brother, you better not think about taking that spot away from me!" Nathenial roared at his elder brother.

"Oh, you wish brother, but no matter what happens even if the world ends, I shall be one sleeping over there cause I born a minute earlier than you," Raymond was fired up.

"Shut up now! May I offer a solution?" Ria was frustrated.

"Please enlighten us by doing so," said the brothers overlapping each other's voices.

"Do one thing, for tonight Raymond you sleep there and tomorrow night Nath you do it. Keep switching every day or if you want Nath, you sleep in my place, I will sleep on the bed facing the wall," Ria knew how to give the ideas.

"No sis, why would change your spot? We will be switching don't worry," and the brothers know how to make sacrifices for their sister.

***

The next week was a breeze. There was sightseeing, trying the amazing cuisine and even enjoying new activities – the triplets were having a blast.

***

Today, was the day when Mariah was going to take her daughter to the Royal Rocker's concert. But right now, she had to reveal a secret about going to concert.

"Okay, so kids gather around in here," said Casandra as the triplets walked into the living room.

"What is it aunt? Why have you summoned us here?" Ria asked cheekily.

"Stop with you sense of humor sis," Nathenial gave an annoying look.

"Okay, you two stop giving annoying looks. The reason why I called you three here is because your mother has something to say to all of you," said Casandra.

Mariah walked into the living room with an envelope which she gave to her daughter and then went and stood beside her sister quietly giggling.

"What does this envelope contain mum?" Ria was curious.

Mariah didn't say anything, instead she looked at the envelope and then looked at her daughter, as if indicating to her to open it.

"Mum, say something."

"Open the envelope!"

Ria tore open the envelope and the look on her face was priceless. It would be etched in Mariah's memory for many years to come.

After a minute or two of complete silence, Ria broke the silence with a shrill. She sprinted towards the guest room and slammed the door shut. The rest of the family looked at each other in bewilderment. It was not normal for Ria to act like this, but probably she just didn't like the idea of openly showing her emotions, especially when some people call her stonehearted.

***

Ria lay in bed as she saw the ticket. It was a ticket for the concert her favorite band, The Royal Rockers!

"Oh My God! This is the best vacation ever!" Ria turned in her bed with a huge smile.

While Ria was tossing and turning in the bed with a mix of smile and tears, the family back in the lounge room were processing Ria's reaction.

"Well, that was unexpected…," said Nathenial trying to digest the current situation.

Raymond hit his younger brother on the head and said, "Are you a complete idiot? Or don't you understand our baby sister?"

"Well, Raymond say sorry to your younger brother. Also, I assume Ria doesn't want to show her emotions in front of everyone. She is probably too shy to show it," Mariah said.

Casandra just stood there laughing at her sister and nephews. She was enjoying their little squabble.

"Why don't you go and talk to your sister about her feelings?" Casandra suggested.

***

The boys knocked at the door patiently waiting for an answer but they didn't receive any response.

"Woohoo! Yes! I am going to Royal Rockers concert! Im Yae-Joon, my bias here I come!" Ria was basically singing out sentences and randomly dancing around.

"Yup there we go brother! We just needed to wait for this…," Nathenial was saying listening to his sister going bananas on the other side of the door.

"Shall we knock again?" Raymond asked.

Nathenial nodded. The brothers knocked again, and this time they got a response, to which they responded by entering the room.

"What the heck!?" Nathaniel exclaimed seeing his sister jumping around, while tossing her clothes here and there.

"I am so sorry; I didn't notice you guys there!" Ria said.

"Why did you run away like that from the living room?" Raymond questioned.

"Well, I am not that sort of a person who would openly show her feelings in public, whether it may be around family or friends." Ria replied.

Raymond and Nathaniel chuckled at their sister's sentence.

"There's nothing to chuckle about you two…" Ria said with an annoyed look on her face.

***

While the triplets were having a conversation their mother and aunt were eavesdropping.

"I suppose she is very excited," Casandra said.

" You read Ria perfectly."

***

Waiting for the sunset and evening to arrive felt like an eternity to our impatient Ria. After lunch, the entire afternoon was spent by Ria choosing her outfit for the concert.

"I guess this is the one." Ria said picking up her favorite torn black baggy jeans and oversized t-shirt with a black bucket hat with patterns on it.

"At last somebody finally decided their outfit after spending the entire afternoon locked up within these four walls…," a female voice spoke from the back.

"Sure, did mum. As a fangirl it is not easy to choose the proper outfit…" Ria ended her sentence with a bit of French accent.

"Get ready, we will leave within 2 minutes." Mariah said.

***

"Someone surely is in a concert mood…" Raymond greeted his baby sister.

"Hahaha yes." Ria smiled and replied.

A car honk was a sign that it was time to go. Ria ran and sat in the car, while Mariah bid the goodbye to the boys and left too.

"So, it's only Aunt Casandra, you and me tonight I suppose." Nathaniel said.

"Yeah…" Raymond added.

"Why don't you boys watch a movie and play video games while I order food from outside for you two. And after dinner we can go out for dessert," Cassandra suggested.

The brothers smiled and began watching an action movie. They boys spent 2 hours watching the film and then they played video games until their dinner arrived.

"Dinner has arrived boys!" Casandra called out.

Both the brothers let go of the console and sat with their aunt to have a hearty meal with long conversations.

"So Raymond how is it like to be the leader of Varsity?" Casandra asked

"It is tough and fun. There are responsibilities and sometimes fun…" Raymond replied

"Sometimes???" Nathaniel gave a weird look to his elder brother.

"Okay fine let me rephrase, it is half and half; responsibilities and fun." Raymond rephrased.

Nathaniel and Casandra laughed. Raymond on the other hand was embarrassed and continued eating, look down at his plate.

***

Back in their room, the brothers were getting ready to go out with their aunt for dessert. While Nathaniel was changing, Raymond was silently scrolling through his phone.

"Hmmm…" Raymond sighed

"What happened brother?" Nathaniel questioned his brother.

"Don't talk to me Nathaniel!" Raymond was angry.

"I am sorry for embarrassing you in front of aunt." Nathaniel understood his brother's anger.

"It is alright. I also shouldn't have taken this small joke too seriously."

Both the brothers headed out of the room with a bright smile on their faces and went down in the living room where their aunt was eagerly waiting for them.

"What took you two so long? For a moment I thought that you two weren't going to show up at all." Casandra said.

"Nothing, we were just having a small talk amongst ourselves," Raymond replied.

"Alright no problem. Now that you two are here let's head out for dessert."

"Any idea when mum and sis are going to be back?" Nathaniel questioned.

"Mariah just called. She said that the concert was over an hour ago and she and Ria are now having dinner and will meet us directly at the dessert café."

***

In the car, there an awkward silence between the aunt and nephews and why not? After all, they had lost contact for many years.

"So how do you two like South Korea so far?" Casandra spoke to end the silence.

"It is amazing. Since Ria had always been cribbing and making a fuss about coming to Seoul so we always had to do a lot of research on local sites about the places, cuisines, tourist attractions, etc." Nathaniel said.

"Well, at least her years of dream has finally come true. Thanks to you aunt." Raymond added while smiling.

"It seems you two really loved South Korea." Casandra understood her nephew's words.

"What is the thing you guys liked the most?" Casandra questioned.

"Parasailing!" Both the brothers replied in a union.

"Well, don't you get to do parasailing back at home?" Casandra was curious.

"No." Nathaniel replied.

"Miss. Casandra, we have arrived at the destination." The driver said stopping the car in front of a huge dessert café.

***

Mariah and Ria were sitting on the sofa and waiting for the others to arrive. When Casandra, Raymond and Nathaniel arrived, Ria noticed and waved at them signaling them to come and sit.

"So, how was the concert?" Nathaniel asked in a singing way.

"It was amazing, the cheers filled the auditorium and Ria revealed her fangirl side, and she had a different vibe on." Mariah said watching her daughter blush and her cheeks turning red.

"Mum, stop!" Ria hid her face in her palms.

"Ria, why don't you help me choose ice cream flavors for your brothers." Casandra interrupted.

"Sure aunt." Ria got up and walked to the counter and saw all the different flavors and selected her brothers favorite flavors along with hers. Meanwhile, Casandra chose the flavor which she and Mariah used to love as kids.

"That will be $30," said cashier."

Casandra paid the amount while Ria took all the ice creams and went back to where her mum and brothers were sitting.

"Enjoy your ice cream everyone!" Ria said cheekily.

A cheery mood was floating around everyone. This trip was the most memorable of all for the entire family. But now they had to head back home and get ready to embrace their normal busy life.

THE END

Chapter 6 – Teenagers and Saviors

Back from the Long Relaxing Break. The Walker Family is now back in Town and the Heroes must Prep themselves for their Upcoming Hurdles ...

The family was back in town with sweet and happy memories of their trip. Ria was typing on her laptop, while Nathaniel and Raymond were discussing something and Mariah preparing food for dinner.

"It sure was an amazing trip. But I was most content to see my family smile and live their lives to the fullest. I hope we can go on more exciting trips and keep creating new and happy memories with each other. Signing off your hero, Ria." Ria finished typing on her laptop.

"What have you been typing?" Nathaniel asked.

"I just finished updating my South Korea adventures on my online blog." Ria smiled and replied.

Nathaniel shifted to where his sister was sitting and took her laptop and began reading her blog.

"You are a master of words Ria. Reading your blog feels like experiencing everything once again without even being there physically." Raymond was impressed by his sister's choice of words.

"I cannot agree more. You do have a gift of playing with words." Nathaniel smiled.

"You sure get it from me; after all even I am a master of word play," Raymond chuckled.

"Yeah sure, wasn't it you who lost in the story writing competition last year? Hadn't it been for me, Bay City high would have lost its most prestigious awards." Ria laughed.

Ria suddenly ran around the dining table as Raymond pretended to chase after her. Laughter rang throughout the house.

"Stop it you two. Gosh! You two are worse than the neighbors' cats. Even they don't run around the alley chasing each other like you two do," Mariah said as she placed the dishes on the table.

Suddenly both Ria and Raymond began sulking at their mother's words and Nathaniel came to console them.

"True, but at least they cause less damage compared to the neighbors' cats. Those two ran around the alley the other day knocking off an old woman and she was angry at the owner." Nathaniel's weird way of consolation and agreeing surely bought a wave of calmness.

The siblings sat at the table, and this time Mum started squabbling over a piece of cake.

"Brother, I said I would have the last piece of this cake!" Nathaniel said.

"No way. I am the eldest, thus I shall have it." Raymond said. He leaned forward to take the last slice.

"Okay, I guess it is time for me to be mature. Listen, I have two pieces with me, and that last piece makes it three, so let us do one thing, Nath you can take a piece from me, Ray, you can take one from me, and I shall take the last piece. Happy?" Ria smiled cheekily.

"Wise and mature decision, proud of you, my daughter!" Mariah smiled.

The rest of the day was uneventful. It was the last week of their break, thus the siblings spent time doing things they loved the most. Ria went out with her girl gang called the fearless friends while the boys played soccer till dinner time.

***

"Today, was fun! How about us boys go and watch a movie?" asked Kamran as he wiped sweat off his forehead.

"Sounds fun!" the other three exclaimed as they finished drinking water.

As the boys caught their breath they headed back home, riding their bicycles.

***

"Hello who's this?" Ria spoke over the phone and waved at her brothers as she saw them entering.

The boys waved back and ran upstairs to take a shower. Nathaniel used his mother's bathroom to take a shower while Raymond used his own bathroom.

"Hello Ria, I am Ashley. Can I speak to your mother please?"

Ashley was Mariah's best friend and they also worked at the same hospital.

"Oh, Hi Miss Ashley! How are you?"

"I am fine dear! How are you doing?"

"I am fine. Just wait a second, I am handing over the phone to mum," Ria replied.

Ria kept the line on hold and headed towards her mother's bedroom and knocked on the door.

"Mum! You have call!"

"Come in darling!" said Mariah.

Ria entered the room and handed her the phone and headed out of the room shutting the door behind her.

"Ah…" a light moan escaped Ria's mouth as she placed her hand on her forehead.

"What is wrong with me suddenly?" Ria thought to herself.

Ria went and sat on the couch shutting her eyes. That is when she had a strange vision. The vision was dark and the surrounding was filled with the smell of death, while the only sound heard was the screeching sounds of strange black flying creatures with piercing with red eyes.

***

While the vision was still active, Nathaniel saw his sister with her eyes shut, palms on her forehead, and rivers of sweat covering her from head to toe. Panic ran over him and he immediately ran towards his sister.

"Hey! Are you alright?" Nathaniel was concerned, very concerned.

"Huh!" Ria suddenly opened her eyes and was breathing heavily.

In the meantime Raymond arrived to see that Ria was breathing heavily.

"What happened? Why are you breathing so heavily?" Raymond asked.

"Nothing…" Ria tried to avoid her brothers' question because she didn't want to worry them.

Raymond and Nathaniel felt that their sister was concealing something from them thus they first calmed her down and then spoke again, "Sis, don't keep us in the dark. This wasn't something ordinary. Please tell us." Raymond patted his sister's back.

"Can we have this conversation in my room after dinner? For now, let's not worry mum because she's in a very cheery mood." Ria said after calming down.

The brothers nodded and kept their mouth shut about what happened and temporarily tried to forget the incident.

"Well, now that everyone has eaten, how about boys do the dishes and Ria takes out the trash while I clean the table?" Mariah said, placing her spoon back on the plate.

"Sure mum!" the triplets replied in a unison.

Everyone got into action with their assigned duties and the triplets then gathered in Ria's room.

***

"So, tell us. What had happened to you before dinner?" questioned Nathaniel.

Ria took a deep breath and exhaled out. She was hesitant about sharing the vision fact, but she knew that she had to because it most likely had a deep connection with the Tech Teens.

"Is it something serious? Or do you want to share the information tomorrow?" Raymond asked.

"It was a vision…" Ria replied shakily.

***

"What do you mean by vision?" Raymond was curious.

Nathaniel and Raymond looked at each other with baffled looks on their faces and then back at Ria.

"It was a dark place and it smelled of death and the only sound which could be heard in the background was the screeching sound of weird black flying creatures with red eyes." Ria continued.

"Do you think it has something to do with us?" Raymond asked.

"Yes, I suppose this is going to be our new upcoming danger."

Ria knew that clouds of danger were slowly closing in. She knew that it was finally time to re-assemble 'The Tech Teens' and discuss this matter.

"We must talk it out with the others." Nathaniel said while wondering what the vision meant.

"Hmmm… I agree with you"

"Was their anything else you saw except the place?" Raymond asked.

Ria thought for while…

"No…" Ria replied.

"It is alright. For now, let's go to bed and tomorrow we all shall discuss it with the others."

Ria nodded and the triplets wished each other good night and went to their respective rooms. But Ria was awake till 2 am scrolling through her phone as she was troubled by the vision.

***

Mariah and the boys woke up at their usual time of 8 am. As Mariah was making breakfast, Raymond came down and started searching for their sister.

"Well, where is the youngest member of the family?" Raymond questioned while yawning.

"She is either taking a shower or she is still brushing her teeth with her eyes half closed," Nathaniel replied with a giggle.

"Hahaha, very funny brother. We should probably go and check on her or else she will go to sleep in the bathroom," Raymond said with a funny Korean accent.

The brothers knocked gently on the door but did not receive a response. So they tried to open the door, only to realize that the room wasn't locked.

***

"Huh!"

Ria was still in a deep slumber while smiling a little in her sleep. So the brothers kissed her forehead gently and left the room, gently closing the door behind them and went back down for breakfast.

"Where's Ria?" Mariah asked as she saw her boys walk down the stairs.

"Sis, is still sound asleep mum. Probably she slept late last night," Raymond said as he placed a toast on his plate.

"No worries then. I shall cook something else when Ria wakes up," Mariah spoke as she also sat down with her coffee and toast.

***

"Ah Mummy!" a sudden scream could be heard from Ria's room.

"Woah! What happened to her?" Mariah jumped off her seat and ran upstairs to check on her daughter.

Mariah barged into the room to see Ria down on the floor with drops of tears gently falling.

"What happened, my darling?" Mariah asked.

"You had bought ice cream for me, but my brothers ate it all and didn't even share it with me," Ria said while sniffling.

"What time is it though?" Ria asked wiping the tears off her face.

"It is 10 am my darling. I suppose you had a bad dream due to an empty stomach." Mariah sighed.

Mariah continued, "Why don't you get ready and come down I will make you an omelet and then there is a Cornetto in the freezer which I have kept specially for you. You can have it after your breakfast."

Ria nodded, picked herself up and made her way to the bathroom to get ready while Mariah headed downstairs to cook lunch for her daughter.

"What happened mum?" Nathaniel asked.

"Empty stomach nightmare," Mariah replied while chuckling.

"I am sure it was a bad one, and probably we are doomed," Raymond added while letting out a nervous chuckle.

"No you are not!" Ria replied standing on the second last step staring at her brothers.

***

Mariah served Ria her breakfast and returned to her room to resume her work.

"Now that mum's in her room, tell us something," Nathaniel spoke.

"Hmm..." Ria replied.

"Are you still wondering about what that vision meant? And where does it lead us to?" Nathaniel asked.

"Yeah. At first since I was having trouble sleeping, I scrolled through our trip pictures, but at the back of mind the vision kept replaying itself. So, I attempted to research about that place on the internet to see if I could find something," Ria replied.

"Did you find something?" Raymond inquired.

"Well, a bit. I discovered it is fictional place and there is something written about in two famous story books which we read as kids."

"But then why would a fictional place come to your mind and that to as a vision? Is there something which neither you nor anyone of us know?" Nathaniel was still in a daze.

"Can you describe the location, sis?" Raymond inquired.

"Yes, why?" Ria responded.

"Just describe it to me!" Raymond ordered.

"Jeez! Alright, but let me just reimagine the surrounding once again."

While Ria ran through her memories about the location, Raymond got up and returned with a blank sheet of paper along with a drawing pencil and eraser.

"What is that for now?" Nathaniel asked.

"Are you fond of asking questions about everything Nath?" Raymond was a bit grumpy.

"Yeah, so what? It is a good thing to ask question about the thing you do not know." Nathaniel was surely in a mood to pick a fight with his brother.

"Stop it you two!" Ria was close to losing her temper now.

Both brothers calmed down and sat back in their respective chairs avoiding eye contact.

"Well, the entire place was dark, I was standing on a metal bridge with a river of bubbling hot lava below the bridge. On both my sides there were walls of black rocks, and a strange looking reptile, to be specific a lizard, with black wings and it had red eyes. The lizard was resting on the rock on my right. Lastly, there were strange flying creatures, which looked like prehistoric birds flying above my head."

As Ria's explanation ended Raymond put his pencil down and went up to his room with the sheet of paper leaving his siblings confused.

"What is up with him now?" Ria was puzzled.

"I am clueless as you are."

A few minutes Raymond returned with the sheet and sat beside Nathaniel who had now moved to the living room with Ria.

"Where is Ria, Nath?"

"Ria is in the kitchen, looking for something in the freezer."

"Well then, we shall wait for her," Raymond said with a pensive mood.

***

Ria came back with a Cornetto in her hand. Nathaniel saw his sister smiling cheekily with the Cornetto in hand and tapped his brother on the shoulder to signal that Ria was back.

"Well, now that sis is also here, I shall tell you what I have been up to for so long in my room," Raymond said taking the sheet of paper from the table.

"Wow, you actually drew the place fitting the exact description that sis mentioned." Nathaniel was impressed.

Ria knew her brother was talented but also realised the vision felt alive, real. She had a nagging suspicion that something was going to happen, soon.

***

The doorbell rang, and Ria was about to answer it but Nathaniel saved her the trouble of answering it by waking towards the door to see who it was at 2pm in the afternoon.

"I got here as soon as I saw Nath's text about getting here ASAP," Kamran said catching his breath.

"I was just being a couch potato so was lucky that I didn't have to run here like you did Kamran," Pearce said cheekily.

"Why call us in such a hurry though Nath? Everything fine with you three?" Pearce asked.

Kamran and Pearce entered and made themselves at home while Ria finished the last bite of the Cornetto and went to the kitchen to get a glass of water. She knew mum did not like her having a glass right after eating ice-cream, but Ria was very thirsty.

"Guys, it would be better if we have the conversation in my room and not out here." Ria said pointing at her mum's room door.

Everyone nodded and went upstairs to Ria's room, while Ria went to inform her mum that her friends had arrived and there were going to chill in her room.

***

There was silence in the room until Ria entered. Kamran and Pearce were intrigued as to why they had been called suddenly to the home of the Walkers. While the boys comfortably settled on Ria's bed, she pulled up a chair and sat at the edge of the bed.

"Yesterday I had a vision about a location and I am assuming that is our next mission or adventure."

"Can you describe the place, Ria?" Kamran questioned.

Raymond showed Kamran and Pearce the picture he had drawn that fitted Ria's description. Kamran looked over the picture and analyzed every detail with care.

"This is an amazing drawing, but what can we deduce from it? Also, how do we know if the vision Ria had was true?" Kamran shot the questions at his friends.

Everyone looked at Ria for a response. Ria felt everyone's stare and felt uncomfortable, but she had to come up with an accurate answer.

"It is true, because whenever I get a vision my poison level increases a bit. But Kamran you are right, just from a picture no deduction can be made because this place in my vision is actually a fictional one; it is from one of our favorite childhood fantasy books, " Ria replied.

Kamran had a look of shock on his face. How could a fictional image turn real in Ria's vision.

"I think it is best that we make our way to Xandacross and scan the image. I am sure we will get an accurate answer and this will curb our curiosity and clear any doubts we have," Nathaniel suggested.

"Sure." Everyone replied in union.

***

Everyone headed downstairs. Raymond told his mum that he was heading out with his friends and siblings.

"Nath teleport us to Xandacross," Pearce said as he and his friends started walking.

***

The group was now back at the forbidden ferry, were the robot rested. Nathaniel typed a password on his watch and the ferry opened revealing a huge robot, with one foot open allowing the teens to enter inside it.

"It has been about two months since we all last saw you Xandacross. Feels like home again now," Ria said.

"Well, I shall place the picture in the scanner, while you guys can just laze around here, or probably do some equipment inspection, as we haven't been here in a long-time so a few things might not be working at the full efficiency level," Nathaniel spoke as he walked towards the high-tech scanner and placing the picture in it.

The other members began with equipment testing, while Nathaniel waited near the scanner scrolling through his phone.

"What about this glove, there is a slight dent. Ray, can you fix it for me," Ria said, handing the glove to her brother.

"We need to repaint the hoverboards. Also, some of our watch bands are worn out, so we need new bands people!" Kamran yelled.

A sudden ding from the scanner alerted everyone and they walked over to the computer.

"What has it discovered?" Pearce asked.

"Wait for the text to load on the computer Pearce."

Ria let out a cryptic sigh which explained all her emotions at the same time. On the other hand, Nathaniel was dismayed and speechless.

"Illusion matter to us, but then, these are fairytales. When they turn to reality, daydreams turn to nightmares engulfing every bit of you. You are no longer living in fairytale land but become a psychopath in the real world," Ria read the text off the screen.

"What does that mean?" Kamran asked.

Silence swirled in the atmosphere, but then Ria's eyes lit up and she punched some keys on the keyboard.

"The mind reality," Ria spoke the words she typed.

"What is that Ria?" Raymond asked.

"It was a famous video game back in the 90s, and around 2010 or 2011, the game was banned worldwide because when kids played the game, they disappeared and were never to be found again," Ria said.

"But then you said it was a fictional place." Kamran shook his head as he spoke.

"The fictional place in our favorite childhood fantasy book was based on this game itself. Also, when the game started the opening had this very dialogue which was displayed on the screen," Ria answered.

Silence engulfed the air for a while. The gang processes what they had just heard. A fairytale, turned nightmare coming to life. The real disappearance of children. But the question remained, why did it come as a vision to Ria?

Raymond surveyed the faces of everyone as he spoke, "I think we should stop thinking about this for now. It is already 6pm, and I am sure mum will be biting her nails by now. We should head back home. Plus, we have school tomorrow. We will get together again and figure out what to do at some other time.

He then signaled Nathaniel. Nathaniel nodded and teleported everyone back to the Walker's house living room.

***

Everyone was now back at the Walker's living room standing in a circle as they were back there on the robot. Suddenly, Mairah stepped out of her room hearing the voice of the children.

"Oh, you all are back. I shall go and prepare dinner for you three. Kamran and Pearce would you boys like to join us for dinner as well?" Mariah smiled sweetly at the kids.

"No thank you Mrs. Walker, I am going out for dinner with my family." Pearce said.

"My cousins have come from Sydney to visit our family Mrs. Walker, so I better head back home now," Kamran also gave his excuse.

"Alright, see you two tomorrow. Good night!" Mariah smiled at Kamran and Pearce and waved them bye, while Raymond went to see them out.

"I shall go up, change and pack my bag for tomorrow," Ria said climbing up the rusty old stairs.

Nathaniel went up as well after a second and into his room shutting the door behind him. The atmosphere at home was different than the usual cheerful days. Thoughts were swirling in the minds of the siblings. They were not worried about school, they would ace it, but they all had the same lingering thought about a fairytale coming true.

****

"Honey! Come down for dinner. Nathaniel come down for dinner!" Mariah called out.

Hearing their mother call, Nathaniel and Ria silently walked down the groaning rusty stairs. Raymond on the other hand was already at the dinner table waiting for his siblings to come down and join him.

***

There was an eerie silence floating all around the dinner table.

"You two are awfully quite today," Mariah said looking at Nathaniel and Ria.

Ria lost her appetite, rudely pushed her chair back and stormed off to her room, slamming the door and laying on her bed facing the ceiling. Mariah got up to get her when Raymond gently said, "Mum let her be." Mariah nodded.

***

Ria thought, "Life is playing a treasure hunt with us right now. But whatever it is, I cannot let unattached strings get to me. I must try to attach these strings to seek a clue and get closure."

***

It was 11pm, and Mariah came to the kitchen to get a glass of water when she saw her sons trying to cook something.

"What are you two doing here so late at night?" Mariah questioned her sons.

"We are making ramen for sis because she had gotten up after eating 2 spoons." Nathaniel let out a nervous chuckle.

Mariah let out a chuckle and went to the cabinet where bowls and chopsticks were kept and took them out and aided her sons to make a midnight snack for Ria.

***

Ria's bed was filled with books. Some were half-open, while others lay scattered across her bed.

"Finally, after hours of research, I may have found something. Now, I am really hungry. I feel like ramen."

***

The noodles were ready thanks to Mariah helping the boys. Just as Mariah was about to walk up the stairs, she saw a smiling Ria coming.

"I was just about to call you down honey," Mariah said smiling at her daughter.

"We had a telepathic moment mum, mother and daughter bond," Ria's expressions made it evident that she had achieved something great or was content with finding something out.

"You didn't have proper dinner sis, so Nath and I made your favorite ramen and not to forget, thanks to mum, it made it into this bowl!" Raymond exclaimed.

"Is it? Well, I am rather excited to see what sort of ramen you both have cooked," Ria giggled.

Raymond and Nathaniel were flabbergasted hearing their sister underestimating their cooking skills. Well, it was obvious as Ria had never seen her brothers cook that much, despite their passion for cooking.

"Ouch, that hurt to hear. You underestimate my capabilities in culinary area. So be it! I shall gladly accept it," Nathaniel said while pouting.

While Raymond sulked, Ria continued to giggle.

"I may have given my judging comment a little sooner before actually tasting the dish. My sincere apologies my dear brothers."

"Well, I accept your apology but I want you to taste the ramen and then give us your honest opinion about the ramen," Raymond said quietly.

Ria smiled, sat down on the chair, and took a big bite of her ramen.

"Well, I must say, I am impressed but I am wondering, exactly how much did mum help you with this to get it to taste exceptionally well," Ria grinned.

Nathaniel and Raymond shrugged their shoulders and grinned sheepishly at Ria. Ria ate quickly as she had so much to share with hr brothers.

"Well, that was delicious and filling. Nath and Ray can you stop by my room for about fifteen minutes before you go to bed?"

"Sure! We will be there shortly once we help mum clean up," Nathaniel said.

***

"So, what did you want to show or rather tell us?" questioned Nathaniel.

"Yes! I kind of joined the dots from the pieces of puzzle which Xandacross had provided us," Ria was jumping up and down.

"Oh well, you are killing me right now sis! Tell us what you want to show us…" Raymond's impatience was being tested.

Ria took out her laptop from the drawer and showed them a news article that was published in 2001.

"What is this news all about? That is so long ago, what is the relevance," Raymond asked.

Ria looked at her brothers.

"It has been suggested that after that game was banned and the storybook was created, some organization had created a real life projector where the actual setting of the game was shown. But no one ever found that organization or the projector."

"So, maybe what you are trying to say is that those kids disappeared because the game wasn't actually a game but some sought of projection or something?" Nathaniel questioned.

"Well, yes. But I have still trying to find out how true this story is. There has been no such evidence to prove this statement," Ria said while playing with her fingers.

The only sound that could be heard in the entire room was of relieved sighs; even if the theory of Ria's vision was not yet proven, they now had a lead to investigate whether it was true or just another myth like described in the fairytale.

"Maybe, we can start investigating tomorrow with Kamran and Pearce but for now, we better go to bed if want to be able to get up in the morning," Nathaniel said.

As soon as Raymond and Nathaniel left, Ria cleared the book away and then cozied up in the warm comfort of her bed.

***

The next morning, like any other morning, Mariah was looking forwards to waking up her children but to her surprise, everyone was up and down for breakfast on time.

"My goodness, you three are all up and set for school! Now this is a once in a blue moon occurrence for me. Is there anything special today?" Mariah asked cheerfully.

"Nothing special as far as my memory goes mum, we just wanted to surprise you today," Ria replied smiling.

Mum nodded, not fully convinced. Surely, they had something in mind, but whatever it was Mariah was happy that her children understood the value of time – being on time.

"I slept like a baby last night, what about you two?" asked Ria.

Nathaniel let out a nervous chuckle, looking at Raymond's first. On the other hand, Ria was laughed at the scene playing out in front of her.

"You deliberately asked, didn't you Ria?" Raymond controlled his impulse as he replied gritting his teeth.

Ria hugged Raymond calming him down, while Nathaniel boiled with jealousy.

"Look at that mum, first sis provokes Ray, and then Ray plans on punching me, and then sis hugs Ray to calm him, not me," Nathaniel began to sulk.

Ria giggled looking at her brother sulk like a baby, so she went and hugged him as well.

"Well, now if you both have calmed down, let us finish breakfast and head for school," Ria sat back on her seat taking a bite of French toast and her favorite yogurt along with peach iced tea.

***

After breakfast, the triplets headed for school in Ria's car. Nathaniel and Raymond were continuously looking at their sister while she drove, feeling their stare.

"Why are you guys staring at me?" Ria asked while taking a turn for the school.

"You had an accident when you were driving back home, in this very car. It took us a month to fix your car, but after what happened to you, we began to get panic attacks whenever we saw this car," Nathaniel said.

"I know how you guys feel, but I am back and with you guys. I promise I will not leave you now," Ria said parking the car in the student parking lot.

Nathaniel and Raymond found it difficult to forget that day and time, but with the reassuring words of their sister, they could temporarily block it out. The triplets got out of the car and walked towards the school entrance.

***

As the triplets entered, they were smiling seeing all the familiar faces along with some new ones as well.

As the triplets were walking towards their locker, someone grabbed them by their shoulder causing the them to jolt with fear.

"What the heck Pearce, Kamran! Wow, I believe I lost ten years of my life today. Be happy I did not back kick you two," Ria roared but started smiling after a second.

"Well, sis, is correct but no doubt it was fun," Nathaniel added.

Raymond stood paralyzed like he was about to cry any moment.

"Look, at Ray…" Kamran slowly pointed towards Raymond.

Ria tiptoed and stood in front of her brother and snapped him out of his temporary paralysis.

"You… alright?" Kamran asked.

Raymond sprinted away from the group without uttering a word, leaving everyone baffled.

"I will go and check on him…" Nathanie's voice trailed as he ran after his brother.

***

Nathaniel followed Raymond into an empty classroom where Raymond stood facing the window looking outside.

"What happened Ray?" Nathaniel questioned his brother gently tapping him on the shoulder.

"No Nath, the thing is I suddenly couldn't hear you all and my surroundings changed to the vision Ria had described," Raymond replied while stuttering a bit.

"Shall we share this with the others?" Nathaniel wondered.

Raymond nodded and walked out of the classroom with his brother heading towards their classroom.

***

Once, the boys entered the classroom, they saw Ria waiting for them to sit next to her. So, they headed towards her.

"Hey Ray, all good? You just ran away suddenly...," Ria sighed.

"Sorry to worry you baby. I do have something to share, but let's wait for lunch so that I can share it with Kamran and Pearce a well," Raymond said.

"Good morning class! Welcome back from your holidays! So, let us start with a vibrant energy and today, we will discuss what you all have been up to during the holidays," the teacher said to the class.

Everyone had enjoyed the first two lectures, but for the Tech Teens; the best part of school, the lunch break had already begun and everyone grabbed their food from the cafeteria and headed towards the Cherry Blossom Garden.

***

The Tech Teens walked towards the garden and settled near the lake. Raymond was quite very quiet. Everyone was staring at him, waiting for him to say something.

"Ray, say something. Ria told us that you had something to tell us. So, what is it?" Pearce asked.

Raymond took a deep breath, exhaling out his nervousness regarding the situation that took place in the morning. Raymond was the one in his family who did not possess any sort of magic powers. He had just witnessed his younger siblings go through a lot of mental torture with their visions, so for him, it was a new experience.

"Ray, tell them. We need to prepare ourselves for this," Nathaniel pushed his brother to spill the truth.

"So, this morning after Pearce and Kamran scared the three of us, out of the blue, for a moment, I couldn't hear anyone's voice. I could only hear screeching sounds of beasts like sis had seen in her visions, and I was at the same location which sis had describe to us," Raymond spoke as his fingers trembled uncontrollably.

"It is getting worse…" Ria said getting up.

"What do you mean?" Raymond asked, looking at his sister.

"The enemy is approaching us at the speed of light and is mentally trapping us in its cobweb giving us an indication of its arrival. But we have no clue what we are about to face, so we must wait for the next time until one of us goes through what Ray went through today to analyze the situation…." before Ria could finish her sentence, the group heard a monstrous roar and a signal was received on their wrist watch from Xandacross.

***

Everyone arrived at the forbidden ferry, and Nathaniel summoned the robot and the hoverboards out with his technopathy.

"This was a surprise attack by the monster." Pearce said as the team hovered in camouflage mode to the site of the attack.

***

Everyone was at the battle site, and the pilot along with the co-pilot used their gloves to pilot arms movements while Pearce entered the weapon code to activate the specific weapon Nathaniel and Ria wanted.

"Kamran, we need defense!" Ria roared.

Kamran entered the defense mechanism code and a barrier appeared blocking the monsters attack.

"Pearce, Plasma punch!" Nathaniel ordered.

Pearce entered the code and the other hand of robot popped out of the cannon forming a fist, and the pilot and co-pilot ended the monster with a punch.

"Well, that was an easy battle and there was no major damage to the robot," Raymond said.

Everyone was hugging each other, temporarily celebrating, and that is when the gravitational pull became so strong that it was pulling the group down to earth.

"What is happening?" Pearce asked trying to overcome the force.

"The gravitational pull has suddenly increased…" Ria was losing her balance.

Suddenly, a huge black hole appeared below the team and they were pulled into the hole, like tiny asteroids sucked into a black hole.

***

The team fell on hard ground with a loud thud. Their entire surroundings were pitch black, except the lava that was flowing underneath. Ria groaned, rubbing her eyes, and looking around while still laying on the floor.

"Guys, everyone okay?" her echo was audible.

Everyone slowly stirred at Ria's voice, and slowly sat up groaning and rubbing their heads.

"Nobody injured right?" Pearce asked.

"Nope!" everyone responded.

There was a strange aura about this place, not a positive one but neither a negative. It felt like a mid-path of heaven and hell, except the place didn't look like it.

"Where are we?" Raymond questioned.

Everyone went numb, there was nothing but blackness around them except the lava which was a mixed shade of orange and black. Defenseless and weaponless, our heroes had finally arrived in a mysterious location which played a game of chess with their mind except there was no checkmate to this game, but now their survival depends on their instinct. Will they last till the end? Or is it the end for them?

***

Chapter 7 – The Alternate reality

The Earth Swallowed the Heroes, Landed them Somewhere, Weaponless, and Defenseless, will the Heroes Find their Way Out Now?

A group of girls appeared and surrounded the bodies of the heroes which lay on the ground. They dragged the bodies away, but never took their eyes off them.

***

"Where are we though?" Nathaniel asked, getting back up slowly on his feet as his body was still in pain from the impact of the landing.

"I guess looking at the surroundings, we are in the location which sis had seen in her vision," Raymond replied looking around his surroundings.

Everyone had only taken about 10 steps forward before they came across the bridge which Ria had mentioned and below, was the hot boiling river of lava.

"What do we do now?" Kamran began to panic.

"We start crossing the bridge to find an exit on the other end, but I suppose it wouldn't be that easy, as this does not seem like Earth," Ria tried masking her fear with confidence.

"But we are unarmed, and we don't have anything with us to defend ourselves with…" Pearce said.

There was an eerie silence floating until screeching sounds of mysterious flying creatures tore across the sky. Maybe Ria Walker was correct, they were not on earth?

"Well, we need to keep our voices as low as possible so that we do not end up attracting those creatures," Ria whispered pointing at those creatures.

"Aren't those the same creatures you had mentioned, that were wondering around in your vision?" Nathaniel asked telepathically.

"Yes," Ria answered telepathically.

"Maybe it is better if we speak to each other telepathically to avoid attracting any uninvited guests and end up being their lunch or perhaps dinner." Raymond also joined the circle of telepathic communication.

The team concluded that they would use only telepathy as their mode of communication, but they were doubtful whether to move ahead weaponless, because those creatures surely would enjoy eating the heroes as their prey – a hearty meal for them, and bad news for the heroes.

"How shall we proceed ahead though people?" Pearce questioned.

"We will cross the bridge, and search for an exit," Ria replied.

Nathaniel looked at his sister and asked her telepathically, "Without weapons?"

Ria forgot that everyone except her was weaponless and good as dead if those beasts attacked them.

"Maybe I can share some of my powers with you guys until we get out of here," Ria suggested.

Everyone nodded at the idea but as Ria was about to transfer her powers, there was a sudden shock that ripped through her chest and she clutched her t-shirt tightly as the pain increased.

Natheniel and Raymond rushed towards her, "Are you alright? What happened to you?" Nathaniel interrogated.

Ria replied, "I assume, transferring power here is a waste. The aura here is blocking me from transferring my powers to you all."

The girls were continuously monitoring the heroes' body, and they noticed Ria Walker's body shaking like a leaf. They immediately grabbed her by the arms and tried to stop her shaking while chanting a spell in an ancient language.

One of the girls spoke as she looked at Ria's veins, "This girl is a true gift from God. Her veins are the proof, but then we must try everything in our power to keep them all alive as as they attempt to cross their biggest fears."

The other girls nodded, and continued to chant to stop Ria body from shaking.

***

"So, sis, what can we do now? You cannot transfer your power to us, and we don't have any weapons." Nathaniel asked.

"What else, except hoping that Ria will destroy any beast if it attacks or we have to hope for a miracle to happen," Pearce stated.

Ria's head was spinning. She did not know what thorns lay in their path ahead, and how everyone would cross it.

"Pearce, we cannot completely depend on Ria… she will get too tired destroying that many…" Kamran said.

Out of the blue, white colored letters appeared in the black background stating, "Get ready players! Level 1 begins in 2 minutes!"

"Players?" Pearce said.

"Level 1?" Raymond frowned.

"Is it a game?" Nathaniel sighed.

Suddenly, a box fell out from the darkness.

Everyone walked over to the box, with Ria in the lead.

"Guys, be careful. This could be bomb." Ria warned everyone and kneeled to open the box while the boys were about 3 ft. behind her, and ready to run.

"Well, as it turns out; the lord has answered Pearce's prayers," Ria said in a joyful voice.

Everyone walked towards Ria, and noticed that the box was filled with guns, a belt, and a laser.

"Well, it seems, sis will be burden-free from trying to protect us," Nathaniel's smirk was quickly dissolved by Ria's death stare.

"I will never feel burdened when it comes to save you guys. Instead, I will be very content and even be ready to die for you guys," Ria said.

Hearing the word 'die' both the brothers hugged their sister. It brought back memories when they watched Ria die in front of their eyes.

"Do not ever mention about dying in front of us. It is something we are now much more afraid of then ever," Raymond said.

"I am sorry…" Ria let out a light chuckle and wrapped her arms around her brothers and stayed like that for a moment before they realized their friends were staring at them in an awe.

"It is alright to have feelings guys," Kamran teased.

Everyone's mood lightened up before entering the battlefield. But this mood did not last long, everyone except Ria started bickering on who takes what weapons.

"I shall take the gun, because I deal with the weapons for the robot too!" Pearce roared.

The others were offended by Pearce's words.

"End it idiots!" Ria's outburst was enough to silence everyone.

Everyone stood still like mannequins staring at Ria. Ria proceeded to hand out the weapons.

"The glove and small rod would be perfect for Pearce, while the belt and glove for Kamran, and as for Nathaniel and Raymond, you two take the small light sticks and bands," Ria said handing them their designated weapons.

Ria stopped talking; and saw the last item in the box which was a belt with small tubes kept in a holder attached to the belt and took it, tying it around her waist.

"What do you think these tubes are meant for?" Nathaniel asked.

"I guess there some sort of bombs or explosives?" Raymond answered.

"Hmm, maybe we will find out what all of our weapons do when we come across some action," Ria replied in an unsure voice.

"Well, then let us begin with our quest!" Ria said not knowing what lay ahead.

***

The heroes began crossing the bridge, the first few minutes of the crossing was smooth sailing but after they finished crossing a quarter way of the bridge they noticed that some parts of the bridge was either broken or was missing a few tiles.

"Well, now what shall we do?" Kamran asked turning back to see if they could walk back.

"No point looking back now Kamran, if we turn back, we will never be able to make it out of here. So, we need to keep going ahead," Ria said analyzing the path ahead.

"Look, those broken tiles; they are actually broken; they might be invisible…" Ria said as her hands suddenly turned red.

"How do we see those tiles then?" Raymond asked looking at his sister who slowly bent down.

"What is she trying to do?" Kamran whispered to the other boys.

"Ah!" Ria cried out.

The boys were also on their knees now.

"What happened to you?" inquired Pearce.

"It feels like there is some sort of boiling liquid somewhere; and unknowingly I placed my hand there." Ria said as she pointed to her very bright red right hand.

The brothers took the burnt hand and slowly blew air to try and reduce the redness. While her brothers were temporarily trying to aid their sister; a tube containing a blue liquid suddenly flew out of the tube holder on Ria's belt and fell on the ground creating ice; and bridge.

"Huh! What just happened?" Nathaniel asked

"I have a feeling these tubes will come to our rescue when there is no way out for us," Ris said hesitatingly.

"Let us cross the bridge before the ice melts." Kamran stated.

Nathaniel held Ria's hand gently as they crossed the bridge safely.

***

As everyone arrived at the other end, there was two doors named, 'Hell' and 'Fear'. Everyone was dumbfounded.

"Well, it looks like we did reach hell at the end," Raymond said sarcastically.

"Shut up bro! this is not the time nor place for being sarcastic," Nathaniel was annoyed.

The group felt dejected. There were going from one hell to another with no end in sight.

"Well, we don't have much time to spare; we need to choose our paths," Nathaniel said.

Ria thought, *"It would be better for my brothers to go for fear; hell would be painful but then fears are equal too. Ugh! Give me a way lord!"*

Everyone was contemplating what path to choose when a message appeared in the air.

'Based on the last challenge, player Ria will go through the Hell door while the boys will go through the Fear door, and you all must leave your weapons here and good luck!' Ria read.

"No, we are no letting your go all alone to the Hell domain sis!" Raymond roared.

"Yes, I agree!" Nathaniel added.

Kamran and Pearce were just boiling; because they also did not want their friend to enter a domain unknown to them without any weapons.

Ria untied the belt and threw it on the floor. While the boys weren't ready to let her go through hell all alone.

"As your brothers, we will not let you go through that door Ria!"

Nathaniel said to himself, *"Why act like a hero always sis? Just for once listen to us, and don't go there please..."*

Ria just sighed, while the boys begged and pleaded her not to go through that door...

Those mysterious sign appeared again stating, "Hurry, the more delayed the more painful every torture gets..."

"We have no other choice guys; we have to do this..." Ria spoke softly ending her statement.

Raymond spoke placing a huge stone on his heart knowing that the others will not accept his statement, "You can go in there sis, but on one condition; you must constantly stay in touch with us through telepathy. I know we will not be able to come to your dimension if anything happens to you, but through words at least we can help you out..."

Nathaniel, Pearce, and Kamran were flabbergasted with Raymond's decision; while Ria just hugged him acknowledging the fact that he respected his sister's decision.

"Are you made Ray!?" Nathaniel roared at his brother.

"Nath please… we are losing time here," Ria said.

"Ugh! I hate this decision but then what other option do we have. Fine you can go there but you must do what Ray said…" Nathaniel explained his heart and mind that yeah, its fine…

With that false hope that everything would be fine, the team spilt into two teams: the boys in one while Ria all alone. Everyone exchanged glances before entering their domains.

***

For our youngest hero, the hell domain had a different view all together; the surroundings were all red filled with various types of screams and a few shadows playing on the red walls.

"What is this?" Ria said knowing very well that she was not going to get a response.

***

The boys went through a different experience. Their atmosphere was brighter and on either side of the walls, their memories were projected.

"This is very different from what we imagined it to be…" Raymond said.

"Indeed Ray, it is like a mix of pure bliss but filled with agony to an extent…" Kamran added.

"Good analysis Kamran. I wondered how sis is…" Nathaniel said.

Pearce tried making telepathic contact with his friend seeing how worried her brothers were for her.

"Hey R, how is everything at your end?" Pearce asked.

About two minutes passed, Pearce suddenly felt a low whimpering voice in his head and realized his friend was whimpering.

"Boys, wait... I can hear Ria whimper," Pearce said.

Nathaniel turned towards his friend and questioned, "What do you mean Pearce?"

"I have been trying to make telepathic contact with Ria but was unable to for two minutes. but now suddenly I can hear whimpering sounds in my brain and the voice belongs to Ria."

The others attempted to make contact with Ria telepathically and could hear her whimpering too.

Suddenly, "Ah! Let me go!" they heard Ria's scream in their heads.

***

In the other dimension, as Ria walked deeper into the mysterious path, a few clips of her life suddenly appeared to her on the red walls, which showed Ria as a monster and killing innocent lives, and then hurting herself because she felt remorse for her actions.

"I never did all this..." Ria fell to her knees hiding her face in her palms.

Out of the blue, amidst the clips, the voices of her family members played in the background...

"You did all this you monster!" it was Mariah's voice.

Ria slowly looked up, not realizing that suddenly creepers had tied her hands and gripped onto her arms for support.

"What? Mom? I swear I never…" Ria was interrupted.

"No! Shut up liar! You are not worthy of being called our sister, you killed so many…." Her brothers' voices boomed in as well.

At that very moment, Ria had accepted the telepathic message sent from her friend Pearce but was too lost with the voices. Ria slowly began to whimper, as the tortures of voices began to worsen with false accusations of her killing those souls.

"I am not a monster!!" Ria roared but the voices did not stop.

Ria began to feel as if her body was being scratched, and to her horror, she saw that the shadows of the people blaming her were cutting her arm with their blades, and that is when Ria had an outburst of her ice powers causing all the voices and shadows to turn into lifeless ice sculptures.

***

The boys panicked as they did not receive any response from Ria, who was just whimpering and screaming her lungs out a minutes ago.

"Sis!" Nathaniel's voice echoed throughout the echoes of the hall.

***

Ria suddenly felt someone was speaking in her head, and a realization struck her that she was in telepathic contact with her brothers since the voice incident.

"I am fine guys," Ria replied while chuckling to herself.

"Thank the lord! But what had happened to you? Why were you screaming?" Kamran inquired.

"Once we come out of the dimension, I will tell you guys…" Ria answered.

Everything was silent, until Ria told the boys that they should not worry too much about her and instead move ahead and find an exit out of the dimension.

***

The boys were slightly relieved that Ria was fine now, and that they had to continue moving ahead to find their way out of the dimension.

"So, we have been walking for almost an hour. And nothing has happened so far…" Kamran said.

"Well, it is good thing for us. The quicker we move the better…" Nathaniel said.

"Well, maybe we were too much into our heads boys…" shivers ran down Raymond's spine, as he pointed ahead.

Everyone was flabbergasted seeing the scene ahead of them. As shivers now ran down everyone's spine, they all tip-toed two steps back.

Nathaniel started a telepathic communication with his comrades, "What, what the heck is that?"

"Dimension name fear… obviously, it has something to do with our fears…" Pearce replied.

"Our common fear to be specific…" Pearce felt lumps of words stuck in his throat as he shuddered.

Everyone covered their noses and slowly began to move forward.

"Let us talk about our situation…" Nathaniel said uncovering his nose.

The boys stood there hearing all the screams of the same person being tortured in different ways.

"This will not be that easy for us…" Raymond said closing his eyes trying to block out the screams.

"Sis, don't die…" Nathaniel prayed.

"The challenge won't be easy; if you can shatter the illusion, then you cross it or else die with the guilt of being unable to save your loved ones when you have the power to do so," an icy voice whispered.

The boys were startled. They looked around only to realize there was no one there.

"Who was it?" Kamran inquired with the others.

"It was the answer to our question…" Pearce answered.

The boys were stumped. They just looked at one another shaking their heads. It is then that they received a telepathic message from Ria.

***

Ria was clearing her hurdles and was a mile away from the exit. She could hear everyone feeling scared and trying to decipher the riddle.

"Guys..."

The boys were relieved.

"It feels like we have not heard your voice for centuries sis. How are you holding up?" Raymond said feeling his eyes brim up with tears.

Ria chuckled to herself hearing her brother's statement.

"The challenges are much tougher than I expected, but you know me. Well, how about you guys? Is everything alright at your end?" Ria asked.

"Well, we have a riddle on our plate, and we are unable to decipher it," Pearce said.

"Share the riddle, maybe I can assist you guys?" Ria replied.

To which Kamran replied, *"The challenge won't be easy; if you can shatter the illusion then you cross it or else die with the guilt of being unable to save your loved one when you have the power to do so."*

"Hmmm... give me a second ..." Ria said as she continued walking and noticed that the exit was not too far now.

Ria answered the poem, *"The answer to the poem is your mind."*

"What an absurd answer," thought Nathaniel.

"Would you mind explaining the answer, because it feels absurd."

Ria smiled at her brother's response to her answer, thus she took the pain to explain the answer, *"Well you see, the human mind is a very complex. Because it can form worlds while we are either conscious, unconscious, or even sub-conscious. When our minds forms/creates a world or scene of its own and if we believe in it, then it becomes our reality but if we do not believe it and if we create our own image in the mind and we believe in that then that would also become real."*

The boys understood the explanation, everything began to fall in place for everyone. So, the boys shut their eyes and imagined the opposite of the scene shown in front of them to cross this hurdle.

"You are genius sis!" Raymond exclaimed as he led the team ahead and now, they were also a mile away from the exit.

"Well how far are you guys from the exit?" Ria inquired.

"Well, we are about a mile away. How about you?" Pearce answered.

"I am also…." The telepathic connection was suddenly lost as a sudden fog obstructed the path causing our heroes to faint.

***

The fog barrier disappeared; the heroes laid unconscious in a glass filled dimension. Nathenial slowly stirred as he began to regain consciousness and he saw a shadowy figure through his blurred vision. He called out to the figure weakly.

"Hey, stop! Do not leave us here..." Nathenial's eyes went black once again and his head fell back on the floor.

***

As the girls were watching over the unconscious heroes, they saw Nathenial's body slowly move, along with his lips. He was talking; to be specific calling out to someone. The girls attempted to look into Nathaniel's mind but failed miserably and all they could do was watch helplessly.

***

A few minutes later everyone slowly stirred their visions were a bit blur initially but then slowly became clear adjusting to the surroundings. Ria slowly sat up, examining her surroundings.

"Where are we? Why did I lose my senses back in the Hell dimension? And how did I lose the telepathic connection with everyone...."

A cold hand suddenly placed itself on Ria's shoulder and she turned around to look. It belonged to her brother Raymond; he was awake and was looking towards his sister; lost in her thoughts. He could hear her thoughts; Ria was thinking aloud.

"You thought we were worried; that we lost connection with you. Do not worry, even we collapsed, just like you." Raymond gave an assuring smile to his sister.

Ria suddenly threw herself on her brother, wrapping her arms around his neck to feel comfort. Raymond reciprocated by wrapping his arms around his sister's neck and they stayed like that; until Nathaniel coughed indicating his presence.

"Jealous brother!" Ria chuckled, and hugged Nathaniel as well.

"Can't I be?" Nathaniel winked.

The triplets laughed at each other lightening up their atmosphere.

"Guys, where are we?" Kamran interrupted the sweet reunion.

"I don't know, I guess we have to wait for that strange message to reappear in front of us again," Ria replied, while standing up back on her feet.

"Well guessed Ria Walker! This is the glass dimension, your last hurdle! All of you were smart in crossing your hurdles in the previous dimension, especially you, Ria Walker! I did not think that you will make it out of hell…" that strange message re-appeared once again.

Everyone was baffled, how did Ria's name appear in the message? Was this a man-made? The clues, were they hinting towards all this?

"Who are you? What do you want from us?" Ria's voice echoed through the dimension.

"There is no point in wasting your words sis, we are not going get a straight reply…" Nathaniel sighed.

Raymond walked towards his siblings and questioned, "What is the meaning of all this?"

Nothing made sense right now, the challenges, the appearance of Ria's name in the message, them landing in these dimensions, and the most crucial things of all; why them only?

Ria replied to Raymond's question; "I am sure the message ends here, does it?"

"What do you mean?" Raymond added.

Just as Raymond spoke, everyone looked Ria.

"Is there something that the message has to say?" Nathaniel asked.

"Obviously, even the simplest of messages are arranged in a way to make it look like an ordinary message; turns out to be a riddle, or an answer." Ria answered.

"Your really are a crime buff Ria?" Pearce asked.

"I meet eye to eye on that…" Kamran added.

The words went in circles in everyone's brains; except for Ria who seemed to believe otherwise. Ria carefully went through every word and re-arranged every alphabet position; except for the word 'Glass dimension'.

Ria murmured something to herself while playing with her fingers; thinking to herself; "Glass dimension; will you all be able to take it? Many died here itself. The last challenge; practically the last life…"

"No!" Ria suddenly screamed…

Everyone turned to look at their friend. They rushed towards Ria…

"What happened?" Pearce asked.

Ria was numb for the moment, she had finally could join all the dots. Everything was crystal clear like the water in the river.

"Why did you scream???" Kamran added.

Both the brothers were just like their sister; numb. Ria was the most secretive amongst the everyone. She always preferred to go solo and be secretive.

"No, now is not the right time to tell you anything…" Ria thought to herself.

Ria snapped herself out of her thoughts, she looked at her brothers with a completely different look in her deep-sea blue eyes.

"What happened?" Nathaniel repeated Pearce's question.

"Nothing…" Ria gave an assuring smile.

Everyone took that smile for a moment; but it was not convincing.

"Well, whatever it is, what did the message mean? It feels like a genuine message to us though…" Kamran said pointing towards the others.

"In situations like these, not every genuine looking message appears genuine. Also, the message meant that this is the last hurdle; where many died; it wondered whether we will be able to make it." Ria replied to Kamran's question.

Out of nowhere, everything around them began to glitch, like a television. Amongst the glitch, trees and sounds of life could be heard.

"What? What is all this?" everyone questioned at the same time.

***

While the girls were watching over the unconscious heroes, they saw everyone slowly regaining their senses, and that they were trying to open their eyes.

"What is happening? Did he let them go that easily? Or was he frightened from the god-gifted one?" one of the girls said looking at Ria.

"No clue, it feels like, something is happening. He will not let them go that easily; he is not the sort of person to let go so easily..." the other added on.

The girls were preparing for their escape before the heroes gained their consciousness.

***

The glitching suddenly stopped. Many tangled knots were about to untangle.

"What was that? Felt like, this is a game..." Nathaniel said.

Back to square one for Ria, she was numb again. Her given hypothesis as if, had found a lighter to ignite it yet the clouds of uncertainty showered rains of question in everyone's mind.

"Back to square are we again…" Raymond placed his hands on his sister's shoulders.

Ria jerked but regained her posture. She did not let anyone get through her very easily.

"Let us move ahead…" Nathaniel said.

Everyone met eye to eye on that statement and they proceeded ahead.

***

As the team was moving forward, clips of various fallen people in this dimension were shown on the walls.

"The fallen people of this dimension… but what is the hurdle we have to cross?" Nathaniel questioned to end the eerie atmosphere and the creepy silence.

"Well, we must continue…" Ria replied.

Everyone agreed and continued moving forward, and to their utter surprise mountains of bones awaited their arrival.

Nathaniel took a deep before he began to speak, "What is this?"

Everyone was just processing everything, while our youngest hero was still joining the dots based on the clues and pieces given to her.

"Hmm… things have started to fall in place. Maybe there is more to what I think. But maybe I am overthinking…" Ria thought.

All the boys were feeling breathless due to the foul smell of the dead bodies, and blurry visions because they were seeing mountains of bones all around them.

Raymond tried to speak while holding his breath was failing, thus he again started the telepathy communication circle, *"Guys, this smell makes me sick! Ugh, my stomach feels weird... Anyone wants to throw up with me?"*

Kamran replied, *"Well, can I join you in throwing up Ray?"*

Raymond looked at Kamran and nodded, while the others were just listening to these two, and feeling the exact same thing; but were trying their best to ignore it for a while until Raymond bought it up.

***

While everyone was walking towards the exit, all of a sudden, a few bones came together taking the shape of a proper human body and began attacking the heroes from behind.

"Ah!" Raymond and Kamran cried out first.

Nathaniel, Pearce, and Ria turned around to check on Raymond and Kamran and soon as they did that, Nathaniel and Pearce let out scream while falling to their knees.

"What happened to all of you!?" Ria was the only one who was standing, while the others were on their knees groaning in pain.

Ria was in a dilemma; whom to help first?

***

Ria was distracted and forgot about the skeleton army. Thus, she turned around and saw that all the skeletons and already fled from the crime scene by the time Raymond and Kamran let out a scream.

Ria was in her thoughts now, her mind was ringing, *"Why is everyone suddenly in pain? And where did those ugly skeleton army go?"*

As Ria was looking around, she saw a whip hurtling towards her from behind the mountains of skeletons. She dodged it just in time.

"Oh, that is the point... those smart skulls hid behind the other skeleton mountains so that they can attack us from there. Maybe it is a time to play small game with them..." Ria snickered and stood there waiting for the next wave of attack to hit her.

***

Ria grabbed the whip and pulled out about 6 skeletons which had held tightly to it.

"Well, tit for tat..." Ria wiped off the sweat from her forehead.

Ria walked up to her friends and healed them with her magic. And everyone continued walking towards the exit.

***

The walk to the exit felt like an eternity for everyone. But they still had to move on because they were now sick of staying here.

"Well, what happened back there with those skeletons?" Pearce questioned.

"Well, tit for tat happened Pearce…" Ria let out a light giggle.

"No other explanation needed sis; we all know from this statement of yours what took place back there," Nathaneil laughed.

As the atmosphere lightened a little, out of the blue, a screen with a logo appeared in front of them.

"Well, you all very smart; but you… Miss. Ria Walker, you are something special. Crossing my hell dimension was not easy for anyone but you crossed it as if you cross hell every day. As for you boys, I am impressed…" a voice spoke to the heroes through the screen.

"How do you know my name? In a previous message, my name had appeared…" Ria cross-questioned the voice.

"This is destiny, you and I are fated to meet each other someday…" the voice answered.

"But it will be boring if I just let you all go so easily… maybe one last challenge shall be enough to entertain me because you all way too smart for enemies but…" the screen disappeared and so did the voice.

The waiting game began, for the next message or for the voice to return.

***

Fifteen minutes had passed and there was nothing.

"This feels like the calm before the storm..." Raymond said looking at wristwatch.

Everyone nodded.

"Well shall we play the brain game till then?" Pearce suggested but ended getting everyone's side eye.

"Not the time and place Pearce," Nathaniel said.

Ria was as quiet as a mouse hearing everyone's conversations. She did not want to give any input as she was aware of the start and end of this game.

***

Meanwhile, the girls who were safeguarding the heroes bodies were preparing to escape the crime scene before the heroes woke up but one of the girls bought something to the others attention.

"They have been silent for quite some time. Did he let them go? If yes, then why aren't they awake yet?" the girl spoke.

"Is it the same fate as the others?" another girl asked hesitatingly.

Each girl stood over each hero and placed their palms face down and chanting a spell in an ancient language, but they failed to awaken the heroes.

"Maybe they are still awake there. The god gifted one, I hope she has the powers to protect the others," the girl said looking at Ria.

The girls stood in silence, contemplating their next move.

***

Ria's silence was now torturing her, she wanted to say something but felt stupid to even open her mouth because of the fear of spilling out the truth.

"Players, welcome to Level 3! The last and final challenge for you all won't be so easy because it is neither humans nor creatures but it is a challenge of speed, accuracy, and knowledge. Good luck! Hope you all survive!" The mysterious message reappeared in the sky once again.

"Well, that is not an auspicious message at all," Ria said trying to sound sarcastic.

"True…" everyone said in unison but they doubted Ria's tone and her silence. She was definitely hiding something from them.

"Alright boys! We must prepare ourselves for the challenge. Who knows what it could be," Ria said standing up and stretching her joints.

Everyone agreed and began stretching and yawning because they were feeling a loss of energy.

***

Like before, the heroes assumed that a box would appear with but nothing appeared. This time instead, a big screen, like a supercomputer, and a virtual keyboard appeared in front of them.

"What nonsense is this?" Nathaniel was frustrated now.

"Our last challenge brother, it could be related to computers I am assuming," Ria replied to Nathaniel.

"Oh, so now you know everything!" snapped Nathaniel back.

Ria was taken aback but she did not take it to heart because she knew it was soon going to become obvious that her brother was beginning to suspect she was hiding something.

"Nath, you are being rude to sis!" Raymond roared at his younger brother while looking at Ria's expression.

"Well Ray, don't you think that Ria has been awfully quite since the skeleton army attack ended, she is obviously hiding something," Nathaniel was in a mood for arguing with his brother.

"I agree with Nath. Ria has been concealing something and I assume she is doing this so that she can be the hero of the day!" Kamran joined in.

"I also support Nath and Kamran on this," Pearce added more fuel to the existing flame.

While Kamran, Nathaniel, and Pearce poured their frustration and blame on Ria, Raymond observed his sister's movement and he noticed how she was analyzing the screen and keyboard as if she knew something.

Raymond thought to himself, *"Sis, why are doing this? Why aren't you telling us?"*

With Raymond's thoughts another message reappeared in front of the heroes and this time this was a different message; it was not words, it was random alphabets.

"What is this? Out of words, are we?" Ria questioned.

Ria knew she was wasting her time and words on this because she was not going to receive any response.

"Don't act as if you are very smart Ria…" Pearce said bluntly.

Ria turned back towards Pearce. She stood in front of him, staring at him without flinching.

"Is that so, Pearce!? If you boys think you are so smart then please go ahead and complete this challenge on your own and leave. Or perhaps I might find another way to escape this place without you boys," Ria stated causing everyone to freeze.

"Fine sis, we will!" Nathaniel roared and walked up to the screen with the displayed random alphabets, while Pearce and Kamran followed him like loyal pets.

Ria felt hopeless and thought, *"I am sorry guys. I cannot share anything yet, because then we won't be able to get out of here."*

Seeing the way his younger brother and friends behave rudely with Ria, Raymond thought, *"Sis, I am sorry I am not saying anything otherwise I will be misunderstood as being bias towards you."*

The tension in the air was intense. No one made eye contact with each other after Ria's anger bomb exploded.

While the boys tried figuring out the challenge Ria stood there with a sense of hopelessness and helplessness engulfing her.

***

Thirty minutes had passed and the boys were trying to decipher the letters.

"Is it something related to playing the name, place, animal, and thing game?" Pearce questioned.

"Obviously not Pearce. The villain won't make the challenge so easy," Nathaniel answered.

"Something related to computers?" Kamran was close to the answer.

Everyone looked at Kamran as if he found Eureka. But still even if Kamran found Eureka, they were still inside the dimension…

"Maybe we need to match every alphabet with digit, you know ASCII codes or hexadecimal values?" Nathaniel's brain began running with the thought of getting out now.

"Well maybe that is the answer!" Pearce said looking at Ria.

Pearce's look described his thoughts to Ria. Ria could not take it anymore but then she also felt happy that at least everyone figured out the challenge without her.

"Well then since we know how ASCII codes work let us start working," Pearce said.

***

As all the boys began typing away random things on the keyboard and pressed enter, a blade came flying towards them out of nowhere and Ria stopped it with her powers.

"Thank you, sis," Raymond said with a smile.

Nathaniel, Kamran, and Pearce were no less grateful, but then something again stoked them and their mean looks returned.

"Well, that did not end well…" Raymond stated.

As the boys continued to search for a solution, a timer appeared in with a sentence that read: 'You snooze you lose!'.

"We have only 59 seconds boys, we need find a clue," Kamran warned.

Ria knew she had to jump in to save the day. As the boys continued bickering about possible solutions, Ria stepped in front of the keyboard and started typing.

"What do you think you are doing?" Natheniel asked angrily.

Before Ria could reply, fog mysteriously appeared and everyone fell unconscious.

***

The girls who had been watching over the bodies noticed that the bodies were beginning to move slightly. They fled the scene before they could be caught and interrogated.

"Take care, the gifted one. Protect everyone!" one of girls said taking one last look at Ria as she ran away.

***

The Tech teens woke up finding themselves in Xandacross's medical room a sticky note stuck to the message board.

Ria got up from her bed and began reading the notes, "Take care team! Good luck with your quests!"

The boys also gathered behind Ria and read the note silently, while untangling those strings of questions that were looming in their minds.

"What happened back there? We fell to the group and now we are here…" Pearce said rubbing his head.

"Guys, I have to explain something to all of you…" Ria interrupted her friend's statement.

"Yeah, sis go on…" Raymond said.

The boys sat on the couch in a circle impatiently waiting to hear their friend's explanation.

"Well, that message which I had re-arranged back there was actually the truth…" Ria spoke.

"What do you mean sis?" Nathaniel asked softly.

"I mean, remember all those kids disappeared playing that game. That was the statement. 'They died in the glass dimension, beyond this lies the truth if you don't believe,'" Ria added.

Ria continued as she saw the astonishment in their eyes, "Those skeletons belonged to those kids who disappeared and died in that dimension. But there is more; Nath, Kamran, and Pearce when you three were attacked by the skeletons, there was a special kind of weapon used on you which contained magic and because of that, you rudely attacked me. Along with that, the last challenge has to do with encoding and decoding. Thus, the decoded message was, "Not yet, there is more."

"But then how did we get out?" Raymond inquired.

Ria replied, "I hacked into the cored database and inserted a virus which shut down the entire system bringing us back here."

As Ria ended her explanation, a video appeared on the screen showing everyone lying unconscious in Xandacross.

"What is this now!? How were we here when we were in the dimensions!?" Kamran was confused.

Ria cleared that doubt.

"We were physically never there. Our spiritual or to be specific our souls were in the dimensions, while our bodies were here…"

The look of disbelief in everyone was unmistakable. This was too much to take in for some of the boys. Suddenly, Nathaniel walked over to Ria and hugged his sister, almost choking her.

"What happened brother?" Ria asked softly.

"I am so sorry that I acted as a jerk towards you," Nathaniel said kissing his sister on her forehead.

"So are we…" Kamran and Pearce also joined in for a group hug.

Raymond did not want to feel left behind and he too joined them. The group fell silent for a few minutes.

"But then one thing is still not clear, why did your name appear twice in those displayed messages?" Raymond asked.

"Who knows?" Even Ria was clueless.

There were many loose ends, but for the time being, they made it out of the dimensions and their challenge ended on a happy note. It was time to return home.

***

Chapter 8 – Being One at Last!

A 16th Birthday, a Special Trip, but the Voice Follows.

30th December

It was a chilly winter morning in the suburbs of Bay City.

***

"Ria is finally 16!" Mariah said, looking at Ria's picture on her phone. "My sweet little girl has grown to be such a fine, mature woman who is like me."

While Mariah spoke to herself, the young boys tip-toed down the aging stairs and watched their mother hum a tune that filled the otherwise quiet morning.

"Mum, we are triplets. We all turn 18 today," Raymond said cheekily.

Raymond also wanted to hum along with his mother but controlled that excitement as he realized it would wake his sister up.

"Mum, I know that you are pretty excited for Ria," Raymond tried speaking in a soft voice. "It seems as if it were just yesterday that we all sat together discussing Ria's 1st birthday, but here we are discussing her 16th."

Mariah recalled those times when Ria had just started walking on her feet.

"So, should we all go and wake Ria up? I mean, it is up to you two gentlemen. Either we wait for Ria to walk down, or we go up and surprise her." Mariah spoke a little loudly as they couldn't hear a sound from Ria's room.

"Maybe, we all should surprise her! It would be fun to scare her, even though she would freak out," Raymond said.

Suddenly, they was a loud bang. It sounded as if something exploded in Ria's room. The three rushed up the stairs.

***

As they swung open Ria's bedroom door, they saw Ria lying on the floor with her eyes shut eyes and a chair also lying down lifelessly like her.

"Woah! What is this going on?" Nathaniel asked, as he gave a confusing look to his brother and Mother.

"Oh! Uhm, Ria was completing her project last night, and she also did not have dinner! I guess she just dozed off while doing the project. I noticed her room lights were still on at 2 am," Mariah said.

Mariah walked over to look at the dinner plate, it was untouched.

Nathaniel picked up the fallen chair, and Raymond picked his sister and lay her on the bed. He was waiting impatiently for his younger brother and mother to wake Ria up.

"ONE! TWO! THREE! Happy Birthday, Ria!" they all wished her loudly.

Ria was now wide awake, and a beautiful smile appeared. However, she looked a little shaken.

"WOAH! You all scared the life out of me! Thanks, everyone! I hope all your blessings always stay with me, Ria said, as her green eyes teared up.

"Our blessings are always with you! May the Lord keep you away from all negativities, Amen!" As they prayed to God and wished for protection and love from him.

"Happy 18th Birthday, my dear brothers," Ria said.

"Now, if you all do not mind, I need to take a quick shower and have breakfast."

"Yes, you skipped dinner," Mariah said shaking her head.

***

Ria wore her favorite, black-torn-styled jeans along with her blue sequins t-shirt and her navy-blue shirt. As she walked down the stairs, she could not wait to give her brothers their presents. She was secretly wondering what they had bought for her.

***

"Where on earth is sis? How long is she taking to get ready?" Nathaniel asked.

"Brother, I guess we will never understand woman. How can they take so long to get ready?" Raymond smiled.

"Here I am!" Ria said.

"Wait, before we all start with breakfast, I want to give Ria her birthday gift," Mariah said as she saw Nathaniel about to put the spoon-filled cereal in his mouth.

"Nathaniel and Raymond, you two hold your sister and don't let her move from here until I return," Mariah continued as she walked towards her bedroom.

"So, sis, any specific gift you would like for your birthday?" Nathaniel asked as he saw Ria taking her first bite of the pancake with delight.

"Uh, frankly speaking, I would treasure anything and everything."

As Ria ate her pancake, she wondered why it took mum so long to bring her present out.

"I am here!" Honey, the first birthday gift for today is from me!" Mariah smiled as she moved her hand forward with a shiny wooden box. She saw Ria's reflection.

"Ha! This is a necklace with a leaf locket," Ria spoke with excitement.

"It is the leaf of love and life," Mariah said, with passion.

"This is from us, our first gift to you!" The brothers presented Ria with a similar-looking box.

Ria opened the box with excitement, and there lay a beautiful locket. She opened it, revealing a picture of both her brothers.

"Wow, this is so beautiful. I shall place this locket on this necklace. I will never remove this necklace, and whenever I am afraid or in trouble, I will clutch on to the lockets to remind me that these are armors protecting me," Ria said those soothing words to show her love.

"Oh, I also have a gift for the three of you!" Ria spoke. She ran up to her room and bought a wooden box and two new sketchbooks.

"Uh, the box is for you, mum, and the sketchbooks are for my brothers," Ria blushed as she gave the books to her brothers.

"What is this?" The brother asked as Ria continued blushing.

"Open the book, and you will find something which is not lost, but we cannot find that time again," Ria said. These words were confusing.

"Huh!? When we open the book, we will find something which is not lost, but we cannot find that time again?" The brothers opened the book as they repeated what Ria said. They saw that thing which they never expected to see.

"Yes, the answer to this riddle is our childhood. It is not lost, but we cannot find that time," Nathaniel spoke with a racing heart and an emotional voice.

"This is special, sis! You are so good at sketching. How could we not remember those days which we all spent together!" Tears streamed down Raymond's face.

"This young boy who fell and stood up again has grown to be a fine young gentleman, a perfect son, a splendid brother, and an amazing savior!" The brothers read with teary eyes and a voice that they would remember for more than a thousand years.

"Honey, thanks! Mariah also spoke in that tone in which the Walker brothers did. This is beautiful!"

"What did you get, mother?" Nathaniel's voice was still the same as he questioned his mother.

"A ring on which my name, Mariah, is engraved!" Mariah was now crying openly.

It was now time for a family group hug. It seemed happiness had returned after a long time. No one spoke a word. The silence was enough. After a few minutes, Nathaniel was the first one to speak.

"Okay, we are too emotional."

"Yes, please finish your breakfast now. How can you children eat cold pancakes? Now, wait here, all three of you. I will be back," Mariah said as she walked away.

"Hmmm, this is the best pancake ever!" Ria said. He laughed in her mind. Indeed, cold pancakes were…yuck!

***

While the siblings were laughing and joking around, Nathaniel thought, "Ria is so mature now. I thought she would be sobbing when she saw the gifts. My sister has grown up."

***

Suddenly, a beautiful melody filled the room. Mariah walked in strumming a guitar. Ria noticed a burning orange flame design on it.

"Wait, to whom does this belong?" Ria asked.

"This guitar belongs to you!" Mariah said. She saw her daughter's eyes shine like the brightest star in the night sky that lights up the entire sky.

"This guitar was Nath's idea!" Raymond spoke, as he saw his sister tear up.

"Why are you crying, sis!?" Raymond chuckled and saw his brother embracing Ria, and so he mimicked him as he let go of her.

"I am, I am not crying. I don't how or what to say? I guess even a thank you would feel trivial in front of such a gift!" Ria took a deep breath. She was shaking inside.

"I saw your birthday wish list when I was vacuuming your room last week. You had left the list on your table," Mariah winked at Ria.

"Love you all!" Ria said in a shaking voice. It was too overwhelming, and so, she cried tears of happiness.

"Love you forever!" as they expressed many emotions and feelings, they all Ria getting emotionally attached to her elder brother!

"Okay, you three, you have to finish your breakfast now. I know you must be so excited to get to the airport. Ria, you must be wondering, where we are going?" Mariah smiled.

Mariah had planned a surprise family holiday to an overseas destination. It had mean to be a surprise for the triplets, but due to a slip-up, the boys found out where they were going, but promised Mariah, they would keep it a surprise from Ria.

***

The next couple of minutes were frantic as the siblings finished their breakfast, cleared away the dishes, and went to their bedrooms to get their luggage. Ria ran back up four times to make sure she did not forget anything.

"I think it's a girls thing," Raymond shook his head and smiled.

"This is going to be our first trip in years. The last time we traveled as a family was when we all went to Disneyland," Nathaniel remarked.

"Memories are not lost, they stay like a shadow," Mariah said.

"Okay, your three, get ready! This is where I feel like a leader." The childish-sounding Mariah ordered everyone to get ready by putting on their shoes.

It was amusing for Ria to hear her mother speaking in that tone.

"Mum, I hope you don't feel offended, but I kind of feel funny listening to the tone you are using today. It is rather unusual," Ria giggled.

"Oh, I am just in the mood to feel happy and child-like again. Let's say I am setting the mood for our holiday," Mariah said, before she burst out laughing.

"Nathaniel, having trouble tying your shoelaces?" Ria pointed out cheekily.

"Oh, you too, Raymond," Ria burst out laughing.

"Stop fooling around, Ria! Come on, do I need to give you a special invitation to get ready?" Mariah asked in her original voice.

"That is the voice I am familiar with! Aye, aye captain," Ria laughed.

***

A car pulled up at the driveway, and out stepped an elderly gentleman. This was Uncle Marcus, Mariah's brother-in-law. He was the brother of her husband, Dave. Even though Dave had abandoned his family years ago, Uncle Marcus was always there when Mariah needed him.

"Why is Uncle Marcus here, mum?" Ria asked.

"He will be dropping us to the airport, sweety!" Mariah replied, as she saw her brother-in-law standing next to Mercedes Benz.

"Mariah, how have you been lately?" Marcus asked.

"I have been well. How are you and your wife?"

"We are good, and also we have a 3-year-old daughter, Hannah!" Marcus said with excitement.

"Happy Birthday boys. How have you brothers been lately?" Marcus asked as he turned towards the boys who were whispering to each other.

"Thank you. We are doing great! How are you and Aunt Sarah doing? And how is your daughter?" Both the boys mimicked their mother.

"We all are good! Thanks for asking!" Marcus spoke with fascination, as he saw Ria holding her brother Nathaniel's finger.

Uncle Marcus had hardly interacted with the family, but he had a soft spot for Ria.

"Happy Birthday, my sweet niece Ria! May the Lord always watch over you and give you the strength, health, and happiness."

"Thank you, Uncle Marcus! How are you and Aunt Sarah?"

"We all are good! Okay, we can talk on the way to the airport. Peak hour starts soon. I want to get you all to the airport on time," Uncle Marcus smiled as he walked over to open the car boot.

Raymond helped Uncle Marcus load the luggage.

***

"Marcus, who does Hannah look like?" Mariah asked as she looked ahead at the road.

"She is beautiful like her mother, Sarah. She has soft blonde hair, and her eyes are the deepest green you can think of. In short, she is a beautiful child," Marcus said, focusing on the sharp turn.

"That is lovely to hear!" Mariah said.

There was silence for a while. It had been years since they had been in touch. After Dave had abandoned the family, Marcus had found it difficult to come over and to make it worse, his wife Sarah was not friendly with her sister-in-law and her children. So, he decided it was best to maintain a distance.

"Aren't you feeling the heat where you are seated, Ria?" Raymond asked.

"I know you very well, brother! Don't try and beat around the bush. I know you want me to sit in the middle so that we can talk," Ria chuckled. She saw Nathaniel chuckling too.

"You are one smart person, sis. I cannot defeat you!"

Raymond and Ria loved each other the same way Ria and Nathaniel did, but this young girl felt more confident around her elder brother as their name began with the same letter.

"Brother, what happened? Do you want me to shift spots?" Nathaniel asked, looking at his elder brother with innocent eyes.

"No, Nath, it is only a matter of a few minutes. We are close to the airport. I can already hear the sound of the plane taking off," Ria laughed.

"That is a way of showing how much you miss traveling, right honey?" Mariah asked.

"Yes, mum. I am dying to get on a plane and fly high, high into the sky where I meet the clouds and greet them."

Everyone burst out laughing.

"Mariah, I am so happy you are going away with your children. This was a much-needed break. May you build beautiful memories with these children. You have raised them so well. I am proud of you," Uncle Marcus said with a broad smile.

"Yes, Marcus. That is why this trip is very precious to me. I love my children, and this trip will be one of undivided attention and love. We will not be worrying about school or homework, cooking, or cleaning. Yes, we will build beautiful memories."

The siblings quietly heard the conversation between the adults. It dawned on them how special this trip was going to be. They were a loving family, and they were going to enjoy this trip to the fullest.

***

"Thank you for dropping us off, Marcus," Maria hugged Marcus.

She saw her children taking their luggage out excitedly out of the boot. There were so absorbed and excited that Mariah had to remind them to thank Marcus.

"Thank you, Uncle Marcus," the siblings said in a chorus.

Mariah looked at Ria. That excitement, that curiosity to see the world had never died, even after the Dave leaving her and the recent events in Ria's life.

"I am so happy that I can finally be the perfect sister and daughter. Let me enjoy this time even with my family," Ria thought.

She had not fully recovered from her past traumas, but she had to keep a brave front – she had to.

"I cannot wait to enter the terminal! I am super excited!" Ria was excited. She could feel her heart racing.

"Ria has never grown up. She is so child-like. I love this side of her," Raymond said.

"I agree," Nathaniel nodded.

However, both brothers had a deep-lying fear that they were unable to express. It was best left buried in their hearts and mind.

***

"Mariah!" That voice sounded familiar. It was a voice Mariah knew only too well.

A thin, tall, fair, black eye-colored man walked over to Mariah. He knew Mariah's name and also the face of the kids.

"Hi, sweetheart! How have you and the kids been? This man asked as he looked at Mariah and the siblings.

"Hello brother! How have you and Sarah been? And how is my little niece?" He addressed Marcus as a brother, and that is when the kids recognized that face.

What a game of faith. After many years, a husband meeting his family and his elder brother. A few months earlier, Dave had reached out to Mariah. He had worked in the Middle East for the last few years and was now headed back home. He had made enough money and was retiring. He had apologized to Mariah for abandoning her and the children. Dave had never remarried, instead, he was married to his work.

At first, Mariah was upset and hung up on Dave. He had called her back a couple of times, and they started talking. They met up for a coffee a few times, and Dave mustered his courage to see if Mariah would take him back.

Mariah explained that it would not be that easy as he needed to convince the children he was reliable and responsible. She had discussed with Dave that she was taking the children on a holiday, and he was welcome to join them. He would be get to spend time with the children and see if this is what he really wanted out of life after all these years.

Dave was more than happy and had agreed to join the family on their holiday.

***

"Hello sons, Happy Birthday! You two are giants. Do you remember your dad?" Dave Walker asked.

"Dad! What a surprise!" Raymond replied but did not offer his hand to shake Dave's, which extended towards him.

Dave smiled, and hugged his sons, and then turned to look at Ria. Time stopped. Ria could hear her shallow breathing.

"Hello, daughter! Don't you remember your dad?" Dave chuckled as Ria stared at him with those big green eyes. His hug broke her silence.

"Dad! It has been years since I saw you. The last we saw each other was after our trip. I really missed you!" Ria hugged Dave tightly.

Ria had many questions. She wanted to ask him why he abandoned the family and why he never bothered to stay in touch. But for now, she was overwhelmed. His hug had broken the spell of sadness.

"Anyways, before it slips off my mind, Happy Birthday, sweetheart!" Dave kissed Ria's forehead.

"Thanks, dad!"

"And here is your gift, sweetheart!" Dave held out a rose gold wrapped box.

"What is it?" Ria was curious.

"Open it and have a look!"

"Oh my god! WOW!!!"

"It is the latest phone of the year!" Raymond said as he took the box from his sister and Nathaniel held Ria before she fell.

Ria was speechless. This was at the top of her wish list. How did dad know this is what she wanted? Why was he here, at the airport today? Ria had many questions swimming in her mind.

"Lord! This girl might go insane!" Raymond exclaimed.

"Spot on, brother! I may go insane any moment! Because neither do I have a clue where we are headed to nor do I know if I can handle any more surprises!" Ria caught her breath and continued, "thank you so much, dad…really…. thank you."

Dave turned to the boys and handed them each an envelope.

"Are you serious, dad?" Raymond asked as his eyes widened.

Dave had bought a platinum season soccer pass for the boys. For the next year, they could watch every match in the private member's area.

"Wow! Thank you, dad," Nathaniel shook his head in disbelief.

"You three only turn 18 once, so I thought, let's make it memorable," Dave smiled as he looked at Mariah and nodded.

Ria felt alive, strong, and brave, all rolled into one. She felt like climbing on a high tower and shouting out, "I am 18 and alive! I am going to live life to the fullest!"

Mariah cleared her throat and said, "Children, dad is coming with us on this holiday. I know this is very sudden, but I will explain more during our holiday."

The siblings did not know how to react and just nodded. Raymond remained quiet. He was grateful for the gift, but he was unsure if he was ready to forgive Dave so quickly for abandoning the family. Time would tell.

After the final hugs with Marcus, the family entered the airport.

***

The family worked over to the check-in counter to drop off their luggage. Mariah had already checked the family in online the previous night.

"Okay, Ria, this is our airline. Can you guess where we are going? You know until now, we have kept this a surprise from you," Mariah said, with a smile.

"The airline is Fly Italy. Mum…we are flying to Italy!" Ria pointed to the monitor above the counter.

"How did you know?" Nathaniel asked, rolling his eyes.

"Never underestimate a girl." Ria winked as she pointed to the monitor above the counter. She then rolled her eyes.

"Come on, you four, let's head to the boarding gate. Even though the boarding is at 9:30, we shouldn't waste our time," Dave said. He was holding the boarding passes.

Mariah recalled her husband had not changed, even after all these years. She blushed and giggled, thinking he had said the same thing when they traveled years ago.

"You never changed, Dave. You are like the water that flows in the river or like the blood which flows through the veins."

Ria caught her mother's cheeks going red. She tried to comprehend what was going on. How could she forgive dad that easily? He had just walked out on the family. Was this called love? What was going on?

***

"What happened back there, mum? Why were you giggling to yourself?" Ria whispered to her mum.

"Oh, when Dave said that we need to hurry, I recalled our first trip. That is why I was blushing and giggling to myself."

"Mum, why don't you and dad walk together? Ria suggested.

"What a splendid idea!" Mariah said as she called out to Dave.

"Hey, what a splendid idea of you to let mum and dad walk together," Nathaniel said as he winked at both Ria and Raymond.

Raymond did not respond. The triplets followed their parents to the security check gate.

***

After clearing security, Mariah and Dave continued walking, and their kids followed them.

"Dave, I want to visit the restroom. It's a fifteen-hour journey, and I am not a fan of airplane toilets," Mariah said.

She turned back and asked the kids if anyone wanted to go. They all shook their head, except Ria. Mariah caught a glimpse of Ria zoning out but ignored it. For now, the restroom was important, but she would need to speak to Ria to make sure she was okay.

***

Mariah entered the cubicle while Ria waited for her near the washbasins. She was clutching tightly to Mariah's purse and lost in her thoughts. She did not realize when Mariah had returned until she felt a light tap on her shoulder.

"It is your turn, honey!" Mariah said as she gently tapped on her daughter's shoulder.

"Oh yeah! Could you hold my backpack and boarding pass?" Ria removed her backpack and handed it over to Mariah. She was out in a flash.

"Mum, can I ask you something?" Ria took the backpack and her boarding pass, rechecking her seat number as she spoke.

"Yeah, go on!"

"I rechecked my seat number, and it says 14A. I am curious. What class are we booked in?"

"That is a surprise, sweetheart! Once you see it, you will know it!" Mariah said as she wiped her hands on the tissue and threw it in the bin.

***

The mother and daughter walked over to the waiting lounge. The three men were nowhere to be seen.

"Ahh, I imagine Dave has dragged the boys to one of the duty-free shops to show them the latest gadget," Mariah said, rather confidently.

"That is an educated guess." Ria smiled at Mariah.

She sat on the sofa near the boarding door, and just then, she felt a tap on her shoulder.

"Woah!" Ria exclaimed. It was Raymond.

"Are you okay?" Raymond smiled.

"I am fine! You just startled me."

"I am so sorry. I was just trying to scare you. I should have known better."

"Where were the three of you?" Mariah asked.

"We went to buy a surprise for sis. Dad felt the phone was not enough. We tried to convince him otherwise, but he insisted, anything for his princess," Raymond said, as he handed a square box covered in a shiny pink wrapper to Ria.

"Woah, it is the latest headphones!" Ria squealed in delight. She kissed Dave on the cheek and placed the headphones in her backpack.

Just then, the announcement was made that boarding had commenced. The Walkers walked towards the boarding line.

***

"I am so excited about this holiday. Wow! We are going to Venice," Ria said excitedly. As they were walking on the aerobridge towards the airplane door, Ria was recording on her phone.

"Look at me, Nathaniel. Are you excited?"

Nathaniel turned back and looked at Ria and stuck his tongue out, saying, "Of course, I am."

"What about you, Raymond?"

He turned back at Ria and waved, "Happy times, here we come!"

Ria was about to ask her mum but saw she was in deep conversation with Dave, and so, stopped recording.

***

"What the! Whoa, this is where we are seated!? I guess I am mistaken!" Ria placed her hands over her mouth in disbelief.

"What are we going to do with this young lady?" Mariah shook her head as she saw her sons' hands on their forehead and huge grins on their faces.

"You are not mistaken! And now sit!" Nathaniel pointed the middle seat to Ria.

The brothers' realized that it was typical for their sister to make an 'O' shaped expression. After all, it was the first time she was traveling in business class, and it was theirs too. The brothers also sat on the soft leather seats.

Dave and Mariah were sitting on the right side of the aisle.

"How long? How long do you think you will escape your destiny? Darkness will never cease in your life. Go on, you foolish girl, go live this temporary life of happiness. Life this idealistic lie, a little longer," a voice whispered in Ria's ear.

Ria sat up straight in her seat. She felt a sudden chill.

"Sis, what is it?" Nathaniel asked softly. He noticed that Ria had zoned out and was staring straight with a blank look.

Ria decided this was not the time to scare anyone. She would have to deal with this at some other time.

"Brother, could you please use your powers to transfer all my phone data from my old phone to the new one? And I shall just add the sim card to the new phone." Ria asked slyly.

"Sure!"

Ria handed Nathaniel both her phones, and he placed them on the tray table. He closed his eyes and touched both phones lightly. Ria opened the headphone box and looked at the shiny silver headphones. Wow! These were the noise-canceling headphones – perfect for the plane. She could not wait to hook them up to her new phone.

"Sis! All of your data has been transferred."

"Thank you, Nathaniel."

Ria removed the old sim card and placed the new sim card in the phone.

***

"Dear passengers, as we are about to take off, please make sure your overhead lockers are now closed and secure. Please close your table trays, and ensure your seats are in the upright position. Also, just a reminder that we have a halt in Chicago." The air hostess sounded like a robot.

The cabin crew went through the safety drill, and once the demonstration was complete, they took a final sweep of the cabin to make sure seats were upright, tray tables tucked in, and overhead lockers secured.

"This is going to be so embarrassing for me to ask my brothers if I can hold on to their hands. I am feeling nervous about the take-off. It has been years since I traveled," thought Ria.

Ria gulped and decided that she would just cross both her arms tightly across each other and clutch her t-shirt tightly. Yes, that would work.

Mariah had read Ria's mind. She gently leaned across Dave and whispered to Raymond, "Hold on to Ria's hand. She is afraid."

Raymond nodded.

"Brother, look at sis. She is feeling scared of the take-off but hesitating to tell us that how desperate she is to hold our hands," Nathaniel said.

Raymond watched his sister sitting with her crossed hands clutching her shirt's sleeves with her eyes shut and head resting on the headrest.

"This is your Captain speaking. Ladies and gentlemen, the flight is about to take off. We will dim the lights in the cabin. Once we have reached altitude, we will resume service. Till then, sit back, relax and enjoy."

Ria was growing anxious by the minute, and her hands were now shaking. Before she could turn to Raymond to ask him to hold on to her, she felt a firm grip on her shoulder. She relaxed immediately.

As Raymond gently pulled Ria's head to rest on his shoulder, he whispered, "It is okay to ask for help, Ria. Ask me, Nathaniel, mum, and dad. Just reach out to us. We will always be there for you."

"Thanks!" Ria blushed.

***

As the plane ascended towards the sky to dance with the sun, Ria eventually settled down. The next one hour and twenty minutes flew by. When the crew announced that the flight was about to land in Chicago, Ria was surprised, how time flew. Ria looked across at her parents who seemed to be in deep conversation. They were holding hands and Ria was not quite sure

"So, here we are in Chicago. I remember Lora once mentioned that her father used to work in Chicago before he got married," Ria said as she stretched her stiff joints.

"Yeah, I remember Lora saying that too," Nathaniel said.

"Do you three remember Lora's parents' names?" Mariah interrupted as other passengers began boarding.

"Yeah, Lora's mother's is Juliet, and her father is Charlie," Nathaniel replied.

Once the Venice-bound passengers boarded the plane, the crew made the same announcements. This time, Ria grabbed Raymond's wrist. As the plane took off, the siblings closed their eyes. Beautiful music played through Ria's headphones as she drifted off to a place of calm and warmth.

***

Later, Ria awakened. She looked over at Raymond, who was reading a magazine. She removed her headphones.

"Hey Ray, could you tell me how long it has been since we departed Chicago?"

"It has been more than an hour, birthday princess," Raymond whispered as he giggled.

"Huh? Why are you giggling?"

Raymond pointed to Nathaniel. Ria tried to suppress her laughter. Nathaniel was sleeping with his mouth open, saliva dripping and forming a pool on his blanket. Ria was about to wake Nathaniel, but Raymond brushed her hand away. He pointed to Ria's phone. She let out a soft chuckle as she positioned her phone and took a video. This was epic.

Just then, Nathaniel stirred, and Raymond and Ria could no longer control their laughter. They burst out laughing, startling Nathaniel, who was now fully awake.

"Guys, you are up to no good. What's up."

"I …can't...I …." Ria was uncontrollable.

"Bro…I…." Raymond was no better.

Their laughter continued until they heard a few "Shhhs" coming from around the cabin.

Dave and Mariah had been watching the spectacle and looked on. They were feeling joy. In his heart, Dave was proud of how Mariah had brought up the kids, single-handedly, and done such a fine job. A tear rolled down his cheek. Mariah gripped his hand.

Once Ria and Raymond were in control of their emotions, Ria showed the video to Nathaniel. He scowled demanding it be deleted immediately. Ria said no. So, Nathaniel grabbed her phone and set out to delete the video.

"What is your pin," Nathaniel asked angrily.

Ria stuck her tongue out.

Nathaniel returned the phone and thought, "I'll get you later."

"Dave, can you imagine how big our kids have grown? It feels as if it were just yesterday when the triplets started kindergarten, then first grade, broke their first bone, started a new sport. Look at them now, all 16 and so vibrant, full of life," Mariah smiled as she recalled their childhood.

"You are right, wife! This bond the kids are displaying is strong. They adore each other, love pranking each other, and continue loving each other. I guess you were, are, and always will be the best friend they could ever desire.", Dave said.

"Dave, now that you are back, I am sure they will look up to you as a role model, too. You will have to give them time."

Dave and Mariah continued talking. They had plenty of catching up to do. He had been away from their lives for a decade.

On the other side, as the couple talked, Ria had once again propped the headphones and closed her eyes. After a few minutes, Nathaniel gently reclined her seat and covered her in a thin blanket. He and Raymond continued to chat.

***

"What is the time?" Dave asked Mariah.

"It is 11:30 am. We are currently flying over Drummond. We still have 11 hours 35 minutes to go," Mariah replied.

Dave placed his earphones back on and continued watching his movie.

***

"Wow! I am refreshed," Nathaniel said as he sat upright and stretched.

"Did you sleep well?" Dave asked.

"Yeah. Wow, Ria is out cold."

Nathaniel touched the screen in front of him to check where there were on the flight path. He turned towards Ria and just caught her head in time before she hit the armrest, which was drawn up. He folded his blanket and placed it on the armrest, and gently lay Ria's head on it.

A couple of minutes passed, and Raymond woke up rubbing his neck. He was grimacing in pain.

"Man, I have a sore neck. When did you wake up Nath?"

"A few minutes before you. Ria is a real Sleeping Beauty. She must be tired."

"Wow, Ria is still sleeping?" Raymond gently ruffled his sister's boyish hair and sat straight.

“Yeah, she is probably in deep rest. Back home, it is so hectic with college, fighting monsters, hanging out with the ‘circuit gang’, I think she needed the rest.”

Raymond got up to go to the lavatory.

***

Ria woke up stretching her hands and legs.

“How long have I been out, brother?” The Sleeping Beauty asked.

“I guess for 3 hours straight?” Nathaniel replied.

Ria nodded and bent down to pick up her sneakers. She put them on.

“Going somewhere.”

“Yes, bro, lavatory. The last time I checked, it only admits one!”

“That was a sick joke, Ria.”

“I know, I’m 16!” Ria winked back.

***

As Raymond exited the lavatory, he saw Ria waiting outside.

“Good afternoon, Sleeping Beauty.”

Ria gently punched Raymond as he returned to his seat.

Once Ria closed the lavatory door, she washed her face. She looked in the mirror. She was 16. A smile crept on her face.

***

Lunch was served shortly after Ria returned to her seat. Ria could hardly eat anything. Everything tasted plasticky. But Ria quietly ate as much as she could. She knew that there was still a couple of hours before they reached Venice.

The brothers seemed to enjoy their meal. They wiped out everything which was served to them. When the crew came to collect their trays, Raymond asked, "Do you have a spare meal. I am still hungry."

A few minutes later, a crew member returned with a tray, and as she laid it on the table, she whispered to Raymond, "You are lucky. I managed to get you a spare meal from First Class. Enjoy!"

Raymond turned and grinned at Ria and Nathaniel, who were far from impressed.

***

Two hours passed.

"Let's play something. Gosh, we still have a few hours to kill," Ria sighed.

"What should we play? We both did not bring any games?" Raymond replied with a question.

"I knew you would say that, and that is why, I bought a game with me."

"You are one smart girl, aren't you?" The brothers smirked.

They played cards for two hours straight.

Suddenly, Ria thought of checking the map on the screen to know where were.

"Seize fire brothers, give me 2 minutes."

"What happened? Why did our princess order us to pause the game for 2 minutes?" Raymond asked.

"Okay, I like when you call me princess, and I ordered to stop the game because I know where we are."

"Ahh, so we are currently flying across the North Atlantic Ocean."

"Ria, I hope you know how to swim?" Nathaniel had a serious look on his face.

"Brother, I will save you. The question is, will you be able to save me?"

The silence was terribly awkward. Both brothers felt hurt. This was not a joke. Suddenly, Ria had turned 16, and she seemed cold.

"Oh, this is the beginning, Ria. You will slowly be changing. It will be subtle at first, but change is inevitable," a voice whispered. Ria was so shocked that she closed her eyes. She could not afford for her brothers to see any emotion or expression on her face.

"That was very cold. I have never heard you talk in this icy tone before," Nathaniel said to Ria.

"Come on, brother, I am just showing off. I am 16 now," Ria said as she stuck her tongue out. She was shaking inside.

***

"Mariah, look, the sun is setting. Please look out of the window. I want to capture this." Dave took several shots.

Mariah had aged so well. She looked gorgeous now, as when she was, all those years ago when Dave left her like a coward.

"Kids, look out of our window. The sun is setting. It is a truly magnificent sight," Dave said.

Looking at his kids, Dave recalled the story of the Princess and The Royal Fairy-tale Family. There would be a different plot every time, but the title remained the same. He observed Ria and chuckled, remembering those stories and the way his princess would cuddle and fall asleep in his arms like a baby.

"What happened dad? Recalling those old memories and stories, right? I have never forgotten those days. I recall fond memories of my childhood with you." Ria smiled, as she had leaned over Raymond to check on her parents.

"Okay, I am bored playing UNO. Can we play something else instead? Like the memory game?" Ria asked. She bent down to massage the stiffness in her leg.

"You know what? Let's watch a movie and then play for some time more and then rest. Lets' conserve our energy for when we arrive in Venice," Raymond said.

The siblings nodded in agreement.

***

Suddenly, there was a jerk.

"Uhm…" Ria swallowed her saliva as she held her brother's wrist with fear and sat upright.

"Calm down, dear," Raymond held on tight to Ria.

"I am 16, and I am afraid of turbulence?" Ria sounded like she was about to burst into tears.

The brothers realized that she might silently sob, so they held her shoulder and comforted her by whispering a few words in her ears. The brothers had started watching a movie simultaneously, and they were minutes away from the climax. They looked at each other and nodded.

"Okay, we shall play the best of x, it can be how many ever chances. So, let us see who wins the maximum number of games," Nathaniel said as he continued to comfort Ria.

As the play began, they did not realize they would play for four hours straight. Strangely, there was far worse turbulence, but Ria did not seem to flinch at all. She was too engrossed in the game. Later, the brothers completed their game, slept more, and soon fell asleep again to awaken to hear the Captain's voice.

***

"Good morning passengers, this is your Captain speaking. I am pleased to inform you that we will be touching down in approximately thirty minutes. I hope you had a pleasant flight, and we look forward to welcoming you again on Fly Italy. And yes, Happy 18th to the Walker kids.

The triplets blushed as the cabin erupted in thunderous clapping.

Dave got up from his seat and pointed to the siblings shouting, "My pride and joy."

***

31st December

The plane touched down at 7:00 am. After spending more than half a day on the plane, the siblings were well-rested and filled with energy and enthusiasm.

"We welcome all passengers to Venezia airport. The weather is sunny, and the temperature is currently 8 degrees Celsius. We wish all the passengers a pleasant stay here." It seemed the voice had changed. This airhostess spoke with a nice warm tone.

"Happy Birthday, Walker Kids!" Dave was beaming.

"The day belongs to all three of you, so seize it," Mariah said.

Raymond unclasped the seatbelt and got up. He opened the overhead compartment and helped to remove everyone's hand luggage.

It was the first visit for the Walkers to visit a European country, except Dave. His work involved a lot of traveling, so he had seen a lot of places. As they all walked past the cabin crew, the one who provided the First Class meal to Raymond bade the family a pleasant stay in Italy.

***

On the tarmac, the bus was filling up quickly with passengers. Mariah and her sons found a seat, and Ria and Dave were happy to stand. Dave firmly gripped the pole, and so did Ria. With his other free hand he held on to Ria's wrist tightly as the bus started moving.

Ria felt something odd. It was like a premonition.

"Mactrack, activate stiff grip on the ground!" Ria whispered in her mind. As she said this, she looked at her Mactrack, her wristwatch.

"Sweetheart, hold on to me tightly, okay!?" Dave said.

"Sure, dad!" Ria answered shakily.

"I see many speed-breakers ahead. I think one of us should go and stand next to Ria," Nathaniel said.

Mariah was staring at Ria.

"Do not move. Stay right here. Ria has already sensed danger," Mariah whispered urgently.

The brothers panicked.

***

Suddenly, the bus was accelerating. Ria felt the driver was speeding unnecessarily. She looked towards the driver and noticed a speed breaker not too far away. Instinct kicked in, and Ria knew that the casualty list would be long if she did not act now. Ria let go of the pole and lunged forward, running towards the front of the bus. She almost stumbled over a handlebar of a piece of luggage.

"Stop! Ria, Stop!" Dave screamed. His scream tore across the quiet bus.

"Go, Ria, go. Can you save these people?" the same voice from the plane whispered.

Ria run right up to the driver, and in a bold move, pushed him out of his seat. The driver was startled. He was not wearing a seatbelt, so it was easy for Ria to remove him.

"I cannot risk the lives of all these innocent souls. I seem to be bound to my responsibility as a savior," thought Ria.

Ria looked ahead. She slowed down the bus as much as she could. There was a slight jolt, but Ria managed to avert disaster. She did not realize that the driver had retrieved a small sharp knife and cut her right hand as he tried to remove her from the seat. Ria brought the bus to a halt in front of the arrival gate. She gently got up from the seat and looked at the bus driver. He looked like he was in a trance. Ria turned and looked back at the passengers and her family.

Ria closed her eyes, only to open them a few seconds later.

"Are you okay?" Raymond asked, looking at Ria.

"Brother, I used my petrification darts to petrify the driver. I will also wipe out the memories of the passengers, except our family's."

Ria moaned in pain. She looked at her hand. It was bleeding.

With the help of Raymond, she gently lay the driver on his seat. He was out cold. He would be in a state of unconscious for a while, but he would have no recollection of what happened when he woke up. Ria used her Mactrack to scan all the passengers and recognized a serious issue. They seemed to be in the control of someone or something, but who? Ria wiped out the memories of the passengers.

***

Inside the arrival hall, Mariah stopped Ria and whispered, "I know you placed pressure on your hand with the handkerchief, but I think your wound is deep."

"Yeah, it does hurt, mum."

"Here, remove your handkerchief and use mine. Yours is already soaking," Raymond said as he removed the bloody handkerchief and carefully tied it on her hand.

While Raymond was tying the handkerchief, Ria moaned softly and noticed that Raymond's eyes were brimming with tears.

Ria spoke in a low tone, "Why are you crying? Brother, please don't cry. This is a special day for all of us. Do not worry, I am not going to bleed out. When we reach our hotel, I will dress my wound. I did bring the first aid kit."

"I feel guilty. Nath or I should have jumped in and taken over that bus."

"It's okay, I had to jump into action.", said Ria.

As Ria spoke the same whisper called out to her but this time instead of speaking anything Ria touched her forehead and tried to act as if she had a headache.

The brothers were shocked. What was going with Ria? It seemed like she was under some kind of spell. Before they could respond, Ria responded.

"Come on! I am fine!"

Ria hugged Raymond and whispered, "Let it go. Let's enjoy this holiday."

As the siblings walked towards the baggage arrival hall, Dave looked at Mariah. He needed answers. What he had witnessed was not normal, yet the family did not seem to make a big deal of it. He looked questioningly at Mariah.

"I know you have many questions. I promise to tell you everything. But I need you to promise me that you will listen and not judge," Mariah said as she tightened her grip on Dave's hand.

He nodded.

***

The walk to the baggage hall was long, so instead of walking, the Walkers decided to step onto the fast-moving elevators. As Ria placed her hand on the handle to balance herself, she felt a sharp pain in her hand.

"Ouch!" As Ria moved her hand, Nathaniel caught her wrist.

"Are you okay?" he interrogated her.

"I guess not. My hand is bleeding again."

"Just hold on to me. You will not fall," Nathaniel said, gently holding on to Ria.

***

Mariah and Ria stood in a corner at the baggage arrival hall while the boys picked up two trolleys and walked to the carousel. From a distance, Raymond saw that Ria and Mariah were taking selfies. He was not impressed. Nathaniel was not amused either. Poor Dave, he did not know how to react. He was still reeling from watching a real-life action movie.

When the men collected all the bags, Ria said, "Brothers, how a selfie or two or three?" She had forgotten her pain.

"How do you do it, sis? How?" Even though you are injured, your face still possesses its shine and smile. You are the best sister that Raymond and I could ever desire for!" thought Nathaniel. However, he had noticed that when she spoke to them, she was insulting them but then quickly covering it up by being kind to them. What was going on?

***

Ria insisted on dragging her bag, but both her brothers glared at her. So, Dave rolled his bag in one hand and Ria's in the other. Our little hero was just following the path which led her and her family outside the airport where their hotel pick-up car was waiting.

"Dad, I am sorry. I would have liked to carry my suitcase," Ria scowled.

"It is okay, honey, no problem!" David gave Ria a warm smile.

The family was booked in at Hotel Aquarius, which was not too far airport. Dave grew up in Italy, so he looked forward to speaking Italian.

***

A shiny, black SUV was waiting at the carpark, and there was a smartly dressed man in a suit holding a sign:

Welcome to Italy, The Walker Family. Dave walked up to the driver and shook his hand.

"È bello essere tornati," Dave said to the driver.

"Benvenuto a casa," the driver replied with a wide smile.

Before the siblings could ask, Dave turned around and said, "I told him it is good to be back, and he replied welcome home."

Once the bags were in the boot, the Walker's settled in the spacious car. Dave sat in the front with the driver. Dave recalled his childhood days and his amazed family, he could not believe how fluently Dave spoke Italian after all these years.

"The smell of freshly baked bread and the way my brother and I would run to our uncle's store to buy a loaf. Those were the good old days, uncomplicated, if you ask me," David said proudly.

"Woah, why did we stop?" Ria asked. The car had suddenly braked. She removed her headphones and looked out of the window.

"Honey, a gigantic tree uprooted and has blocked the path. A few people are trying to lift it but are unable to do so. I am also going, wait here," Dave spoke in an authoritative voice.

"Okay, we will!" Everyone replied.

As Dave ran up to help the others, Ria pushed the window button. She stuck her head out of the window. About a dozen men trying to lift the tree.

"Don't sit there and watch while they are trying their level best. This what you do Ria, help them." The voice was back.

"I am going to help them!"

Mariah turned around in panic. Ria had gone red in the face.

"What happened, honey?"

"Ohh...mum…my brain is buzzing. I have to help. I have to help these people."

Ria stepped over Raymond's toe who yelled out in pain as Ria opened the door and jumped out of the car. She looked around like a crazy woman. That is when she spotted something.

***

"Excuse me, everyone! I guess you all are doing it the wrong way." Ria spoke in English.

Dave was unimpressed. He had asked Ria to stay in the car.

"Ria, how do we lift this tree, then?" Dave asked, with a slight irritation in his voice.

"Dad, look over there. See that thick rope lying by the side. Tie the tree trunk, and you can use it as leverage to lift the tree and move it aside."

Dave translated the plan to the others.

***

Meanwhile, in the car, Mariah was sitting in shock. She knew something had overcome Ria. She thought that at least they would be spared some trouble during this trip.

"Boys, I feel something is very wrong. Is it just me?"

The brothers shook their heads.

"Sis, come back! We can see that your wound has started bleeding again. Come back to the car now," Raymond shouted.

Ria ignored the call. She knew that they were on a family holiday, but she felt compelled to help. She was not abandoning something she had started. As instructed, some men tied the rope around the trunk.

"Listen, we need to make two groups. One will lift the trunk and allow for traffic to pass through. Once the traffic has cleared, the other group will take over to swing the trunk to the side of the road."

As soon as Dave translated the latest message, claps erupted in the crowd. Ria smiled.

"One! Two! Three! Pull now!" Ria shouted.

Using their full strength, they still couldn't lift the tree. As they continued, Ria's noticed her wound was bleeding.

"Mactrack, enable super pull and super grip. Now!" Ria said in her mind as she looked at her Mactrack.

The tree seemed to lift effortlessly, and cheers rang out. Traffic was able to move freely again. Soon, the road was empty.

"Now, part two of the plan. Get ready to move the tree to the side of the road. The group moved to the other side of the tree and began pushing it to the ground.

"Ria, your job is done, now please return to the car," Dave said.

"No, not yet dad."

"Oh god, I am dying. My wound is hurting so much. I have to trust my instincts and my power," Ria screamed silently.

The group safely moved the tree off the road and to the side. The crowds cheered. A few men came up to Dave to shake hands with him.

"Dave, where is Ria?" Mariah asked.

Dave was catching his breath and just stared at Mariah.

"What do you mean, where is Ria? She was right here, standing next to me."

David looked around in the crowd, but Ria was not there. Panic set in.

"Dad, over here," Nathaniel shouted, waving his hands.

Dave looked across and saw that Nathaniel and Raymond were sitting on the sidewalk, next to Ria. He let out a deep sigh.

"My hand is hurting. Nathaniel, I think I need your handkerchief now."

"No!" Mariah said angrily.

She walked to the car and opened the boot. She took out the first aid kit and brought a bottle of water with her. Ria obediently stretched her hand out, and Mariah splashed water and cleaned the wound. It was a miracle Ria was still standing. The cut was deep. Mariah washed the wound with antiseptic wipes and then covered it up with a light gauze dressing. Finally, she spoke.

"Are you okay? I hope it hurts less?" Mariah asked.

"Mum, I will not lie. It hurts."

Dave shook his head. He thought he was the stubborn one in the family, and he was mistaken.

"I think I need a warm shower. I think we all do," Ria said as she pinched her nose.

Everyone laughed. Ria knew that she had to play it cool. She would need to see the hotel doctor for the wound to be dressed appropriately.

The remaining journey was filled with various conversations from the weather, food, culture, and what the family would see while they were there. Soon, they had arrived at their hotel.

***

Dave completed all the check-in formalities and handed Raymond the key card. There were two rooms booked, with an adjoining door.

Before they headed to their rooms, Ria insisted on visiting the hotel doctor. As luck would have it, he was available to see Ria straightaway. He was impressed by Mariah's dressing and gave Ria a small tube.

"Apply this cream after you shower. Your wound is deep but not dangerous." Use this cream twice a day. And yes, continue to apply the gauze lightly over the wound." He handed over two small rolls of gauze to Ria.

"Children, listen, you three go up to the room and freshen up," Mariah said.

"Done, but where are you and dad headed to?" Raymond asked as he glared at his mother. He was annoyed that his parents were sharing a room. Their father had just reappeared in their lives.

"Yeah, we are going to the restaurant to reserve our table. We will see you there soon."

Raymond nodded. So, the triplets stood in front of the steel doors, looking at their reflection, and as the lift doors opened, they stepped in.

Ria was flabbergasted. The entire interior was golden, and there was a red dragon weaving in and out of the walls. It was a spectacular sight. As soon as the lift doors opened, Ria rushed out shouting, "Which is our room?"

A couple walking past them just shook their heads.

"It is 408." Raymond chuckled as he saw his sister running.

"This is it!" Ria spoke with a huge smile on her face pointing towards the door where the gold plate read "408."

The brothers quickened their pace as they watched Ria jumping up and down. Raymond placed the key card on the biometric verification pad, and it turned green.

"Wow! First, business class tickets, and now we have been booked into a suite," Raymond said as he surveyed the large room.

"A suite?" Nathaniel and Ria both screamed.

As the triplets walked into the room, they were met with two king-sized beds, a television in the front, a bathroom with a shower room and a bathtub. The room had a big balcony with a view of the city. They walked in further to discover there was a beautiful kitchen and a great dining area.

"Yeah. It kind of reminds me of home!" Raymond exclaimed as he kept everyone's suitcases in line and shut their room door.

"I need to use the bathroom," Ria declared.

"There is no need to announce it," Nathaniel said.

"Guys, there are two bathrooms. Relax," Raymond said.

"But there are three of us," Ria interjected.

They began arguing about who will be the first two to use the bathrooms.

"I shall go first!" Nathaniel yelled.

"No, I shall!" Raymond yelled back.

"Ugh, fight all you want! I am going to use one. I need to shower and dress my wound," Ria screamed as she walked to her suitcase to pick out some clothes.

As she entered the bathroom and locked the door, the brothers went outside the balcony to admire the metropolitan city of Venice.

"It is so lovely here. Let's pray for an incident-free holiday," Nathaniel said as he closed his eyes.

When he opened his eyes, he noticed Raymond was nowhere to be seen. He had given Nathaniel the slip. Nathaniel smiled and continued enjoying the view.

***

"Who's next?" Ria asked.

"Me," Nathaniel said as he walked towards the bathroom.

Raymond was out a few minutes later, and once dressed, he joined Ria at the balcony.

"Finally, on holiday, away from monsters," Raymond said as he stretched his body.

Suddenly, there was a knock on the adjoining door. Ria walked over and opened it. Dave and Mariah walked in.

"Kids, we have been waiting for you at the restaurant for the last hour," Mariah said.

"Ehh...yeah...we had a technical problem. We could not decide who should shower first," Ria replied.

"That is disrespectful to keep people waiting, correction, family waiting," Dave said, with a cheeky smile.

"We are waiting for Nathaniel. He should be out soon," Raymond said.

"You look nice, honey." Mariah said as she headed out to the balcony where Ria was lost in her thoughts.

"Thanks mum. You look so amazing too!" Ria said, snapping out of her thoughts.

"This dress looks amazing on you, mum. Orange is your color."

Mariah blushed as she looked at Dave. Raymond rolled his eyes.

Both the mother and daughter stood on the balcony looking at the amazing city of Venice below. Ria's mind was still disturbed by the two events which occurred on their way to the hotel. She felt as these problems had been created for her. But she was more troubled by the voice. It seemed as if it was dragging Ria to doubt herself and be mean to those around her.

***

"Let's go, I am ready!" said Nathaniel as he came out with a towel on his shoulder, a comb in his hand.

"No, you are not ready!" Dave exclaimed as he pointed towards the shoes.

"Obviously, how could I forget that?" Nathaniel chuckled.

The three men burst out laughing.

As Nathaniel finished combing his hair, Ria and Mariah re-entered the room and shut the balcony door. The Walkers walked out of the room for breakfast and start their first day in Venice.

***

A beautiful buffet and been spread out. With so many choices, Mariah sat while the rest of the Walkers explored what was available. Raymond came across a table serving special Venetian delicacies such as Risi e bisi (special rice cooked in pea-shell broth), Bigoli in salsa (pasta with onions and salt-cured fish), and Mołéche (deep-fried green crabs). He piled a dozen or so of Mołéche on his plate. After all, he was a seafood lover. Nathaniel and Dave were feeling less adventurous and decided to stick to some croissants and fruit.

As the boys sat, Mariah got up and walked over to Ria, who was still deciding what she should start with.

"Honey, let me help you. Your wound may be hurting you." Mariah sensed Ria was disturbed.

"Okay, but I am choosing." Ria snapped back.

Mariah did not respond. She had strong instincts, too, and knew Ria was disturbed by the two incidents earlier.

Soon, Mariah and Ria had filled their plates and returned to the table.

The Walkers returned to the buffet counters a few more times. Raymond and Dave tried as many Italian dishes as possible. They agreed, this was pure, authentic Italian goodness.

***

After breakfast, the first sightseeing stop was Doge's Palace. The 7 minute drive to the palace was beautiful. During the short drive, the family saw ancient homes, alongside modern homes. The driver provided the family with a brief history of Venice.

He began,

"The construction of Venice started after the fall of the Roman Empire in the 5th century AD. The lagoons were a safe haven, and so refugees fled to seek refuge. With the huge influx of refugees, more space was needed, and so, they drove wooden poles deep into the ground to build upwards. The buildings of Venice are built on this foundation."

He further explained,

"The Doge palace was built in the year 1340 and extended, and modified in the following years. It became a museum in the year 1923."

At the entrance of the palace, Ria was in awe. She whipped out her phone and started recording as the tour began. The palace was magnificent and beautifully maintained.

"Everyone, look here!" Ria said, pointing towards her phone. The others smiled and waved back.

This was a fantastic start to be what was going to be a magical day for the triplets.

***

Their next stop was the Rialto Bridge. The Rialto Bridge is the oldest of the four bridges spanning the Grand Canal. Dave had a surprise in store for the family. He whipped out five tickets.

"This is how we are going to get there."

The triplets squealed in delight to learn that they would be taking an approximately thirty-minute ferry ride to the Rialto Bridge.

***

The ferry excited our youngest hero the most. She recorded the entire twenty-eight minute ride. Ria was so excited.

"Wow, dad, this is an amazing view. We hardly get to see such views back home. It was an amazing idea to come here!" the brothers exclaimed.

"Sis, is your hand hurting?" Nathaniel asked.

"Oh yeah, a little, but the views are just so mesmerizing that I am distracted," Ria chuckled.

Dave pointed out the gondolas to the children and explained their significance as a means of water transport. They were built specially to navigate the narrow canals. These days, they are used as modern taxis –to transport visitors from one site to another.

Ria waved to a gondola as it passed, and the gondolier air-kissed Ria, who instantly blushed. Her brothers burst out laughing.

The family then stopped for lunch at the world-famous St Mark's Square. They unanimously decided that pizza was what they were all going to have. The Walkers were not disappointed.

After lunch, Dave pulled out the travel guide from his backpack and as he and the boys were looking at what to do next, a voice called out.

"Dave, mio fratello!"

Dave turned towards the voice, and his eyes widened. There stood his childhood friend, Charlie. He hugged Dave and looked at the rest of the family.

"Bellissima famiglia, bellissima famiglia!" Charlie said, as he smacked his lips.

Dave smiled and said to his family, "This is Charlie. He is my childhood friend. He called out to me saying my brother, and what a beautiful family you have." Dave was beaming.

"Dave, how are you, my pal? How is life? It has been more than twenty years since we saw each other," Charlie said, in a thick English accent. Charlie was a tall, handsome man.

"I am doing great buddy, how are you, and how is your life going. Did you open up the bakery of your dreams?" Dave asked.

"Oh yes, I did. Right here, over there," Charlie said, pointing towards a row of shops. "I will take you there, but first, please introduce me to your family."

"Charlie, this is my wife, Mariah."

"Your wife is beautiful, pleased to meet you!" Charlie bowed and shook hands with Mariah.

"This is Raymond, my eldest son! He took the responsibility of being the man of the house in my absence." Dave placed his hand on his shoulder.

"Hello, sir, pleased to meet you." Raymond smiled as he shook his hand.

"And here is my younger son, Nathaniel."

"Pleased to meet you, sir!" Nathaniel said.

"And here is our youngest member, my daughter, Ria." Dave turned to Ria.

Ria turned towards Charlie and came forward and spoke, "Hello sir! Please to meet you!" She mimicked her brother's actions.

"Same here. Wow, Dave, your family looks good! Anyways, what brings you here?" Charlie asked.

"Oh, it's the triplet's birthday, so my wife and I thought that we should celebrate it in Italy," Dave smiled as he replied.

"Oh, Happy Birthday, Kiddos!"

"Thank you!" The three responded in unison.

"Let me take you to my bakery. You all have to try my chocolate croissant. Charlie led the way to the bakery which was very crowded. As they neared the entrance, there was a long line just to get in.

"How famous are you, Charlie?" Dave asked.

"Too famous for my liking," Charlie chuckled. He signaled for the family to follow him and he led them to a back alley. Yes, they entered the bakery through the back door!

"Ricardo, where is the fresh batch of chocolate croissants?" Charlie asked his head baker.

"There," Ricardo pointed to a set of trays cooling in a far corner.

Charlie led the family to try some. As soon as Ria tried one, the soft pastry melted in her mouth, and velvety chocolate oozed. Ria was in heaven. She looked guilty at Charlie, and he nodded. Ria had two more. Between the Walker family, they ate about a dozen chocolate croissants!

Dave smacked his lips in happiness. "This is incredible. I am so proud of you, brother. How far you have come."

Charlie led the family past the kitchen door to the bakery. It was a busy scene. The thirty-seat bakery was packed. There were lines of people at the counter ordering the delicious pastries on display.

"We make twenty varieties of pastries. We sell about two thousand pastries a day. In summer, it doubles." Charlie said proudly.

Dave patted Charlie's back, wiping away a tear. Charlie had come a long way.

The Walkers and Charlie headed back to the kitchen.

"Ricardo, I am taking the rest of the day off. My family is here from the USA. The restaurant is yours for today, only today," Charlie roared with laughter.

The family headed back out and followed Charlie. He walked to his Piaggio van. Ria squealed in delight – the van was shocking pink with blue wordings embossed across it: Charlie's Delights. The brothers shook their heads at the thought of sitting in a pink van!

The family squeezed in the tiny van, and the next few hours, they spent with Charlie as he brought them around Venice.

***

A few hours later, Charlie dropped the family back at the hotel. He hugged Dave. This was a magical reunion. He waved goodbye to the family and drove off.

"I want to rest. I am feeling tired," Ria said.

"The swimming pool is inviting me," Nathaniel said.

"I will join you, brother," Raymond nodded.

"We will head up to rest, too," Dave said.

***

Ria changed into her pajamas and jumped into the soft bed. She covered herself with a warm blanket. It was 4pm. She set a timer for 5.30 pm on her phone. Ria closed her eyes and fell asleep instantly.

***

Down in the lobby, there was an air of excitement.

"Boys, we are just hours away from the party. Make sure you wake Ria up at 5.30pm," Mariah said excitedly.

The brothers nodded. They were extremely excited. This surprise had been planned for a while now. The brothers were meant to be part of the surprise, but Mariah thought she better let the boys know what was going on with the recent events in their lives. She wanted to make sure no further harm would come to Ria.

***

At 5:30 pm, the alarm went off. Ria opened her eyes to shut the alarm off and was greeted by both her brothers grinning at her. This startled Ria.

"Hey, no cool. I don't need further shocks in my life."

"Okay, wake up. Come on," Raymond said impatiently.

"I was out for a good one and a half hours. It has been a while since I slept this peacefully!" Ria exclaimed.

There was a sudden knock from the adjoining room. Raymond opened it and saw Dave.

"Dad, what are you doing here?" Nathaniel asked as Dave walked in.

"Ria, go to our room. Your mother is waiting for you, honey." Dave winked at Ria and smiled.

"Sure!" Ria replied. She wondered what that wink was. That was a weird gesture dad had made.

Ria jumped out of bed and pulled the blanket in place and fluffed the pillows.

"Hey, you are not at home. This is a hotel," Nathaniel chuckled.

Ria stuck her tongue out as she walked across to her mum's room.

***

"Did you call for me, mum?"

"Yes, dear. Our dad and I have planned a beautiful dinner at a secret location for you and your brothers. I called for you as you have to get ready. Mariah smiled, looking at her daughter.

It took Ria and Mariah almost an hour to put on their makeup. The birthday princess was confused as to what she would be wearing.

"Mum, which one looks better? The black dress or the white gown with the pink roses on it?"

"Wear whatever you like." Mariah was never harsh on her children; she always gave them the freedom to make independent decisions.

"I like the gown." Ria pouted.

"Okay, but why don't you sound confident?"

"Well, you bought me this black dress..." Ria continued to pout.

"It is okay, wear the gown!" Mariah picked up the gown and gave it to Ria.

Ria entered the bathroom to put on her gown. She looked in the mirror and blushed when she was ready.

"OH MY GOD!!" Mariah hugged her daughter. "You look like me. I guess I should call you little Mariah."

Ria walked over to the dressing table and searched for her favorite perfume. Mum had brought it on this trip. Ria smiled.

"This my darling is for you," Mariah said, as she gently removed the necklace with the lockets and replaced it with a thin white gold necklace with a solitaire diamond in the center.

Ria gasped. She was overwhelmed and started crying.

"Honey, I am not done yet." Mariah took out a small box from the dresser drawer and opened it. There were matching solitaire earrings which she gently hooked onto Ria's ears. "Now, this is what I call a real princess."

***

In the other room, the three gentlemen looked in the mirror, admiring their black suits.

"Dad, can you please fix this bow tie. I have been trying for a while, now," Nathaniel said, as he fiddled with the bow.

"There we go, all done," Dave said as he adjusted the bowtie.

They looked down at their feet. Shiny black shoes polished to dazzle. The men nodded to each other and walked out of the room towards the lifts. Dave cracked a joke, and they all burst out laughing.

***

Ria and Mariah were all dressed up but busy taking selfies and photos by the balcony. A few minutes later, the phone rang, and Mariah picked it up. It was Dave. It was time to bring Ria to the hall.

"Come on, darling, the limousine is waiting to take us to that fancy place for dinner."

Ria took a long breath and walked out the door.

***

While waiting for the lift, a room door opened, and a few noisy girls walked out towards the lift. They were giggling, and one of them was laughing very loudly. Ria thought the laughter sounded familiar. She turned around.

"Woah!" Ria jumped in fright.

"Happy birthday, girl!" It was Samantha, the leader of the Circuit Gang.

"Oh my god, Samantha! Thanks, girl!"

"Happy birthday, Ria!" The others rushed in to wish her.

"No way, Michelle, Olivia, Lora! Thanks, girls!" The surprise lighted up Ria's face.

The lift doors opened, and the girls entered. Mariah was beaming with happiness.

***

Inside the lift, there was non-stop chatter. The girls were oohing and aahing over Ria's gorgeous gown. The lift doors opened on Level 5. Ria was confused.

"Mum, we have a limo pick-up, right? Why are we on this floor?

"Oh, I want to show you something, darling," Mariah tried to hide her panic.

"This is a big surprise. When did you girls arrive in Venice?"

"Oh, we arrived a day before you did," Samantha replied.

"Your mother wanted to give you and your brothers the best 16th present," Olivia added.

"When she told us about Italy, we were stunned when your parents said they would pay for the trip," Lora beamed.

Ria turned to Mariah and hugged her, whispering, "Thank you so much. I am speechless, mum."

The group arrived at a door, and Mariah said to Ria, "Honey, push the door open."

***

Inside the hall, a group of people was waiting to surprise Ria.

"Everyone, quiet. I think that is Ria," whispered Dave.

"I cannot wait to see Ria's reaction," whispered Nathaniel.

***

Outside, Ria felt a wave of panic. What was going on? Mum was all of a sudden so secretive. Ria took a deep breath and opened the door.

It was a small banquet room, but it was pitch dark.

"Come on, is this a joke," Ria blurted out.

"Now!" Raymond whispered.

The lights went on.

"Oh, My God! This is Amazing!!" Ria exclaimed. Her mouth was hanging in shock as to what she saw next.

"SURPRISE!" The room erupted in cheers. Ria was so stunned that she could hardly breathe or move. There in front of her were the male members of the Walker family and the Tech Teens. Kamran and Pearce had their mouths open. They were not expecting to see this version of Ria. She looked like Cinderella.

"Happy birthday, Ria," Pearce was blushing.

"Now, let's start the party," Dave said.

It took Ria a few minutes to compose herself as she learned that her friends had all arrived together a day before she and her family had. There were so glad to be a part of the birthday celebrations for the triplets.

"Thank you so much for organizing this trip for us and talking to our parents to allow us to be part of this special celebration," Kamran said to Dave as he hugged him.

"It was our pleasure. I hear from Mariah you guys have had quite an adventure in the last year," Dave winked at the group of friends.

A few hours passed as they ate and, laughed, and drank. Soon, it was time to cut the cake.

***

Dave popped a bottle of champagne and poured some for everyone present.

"Okay, here is the cake! Birthday girl, please stand in the center, mum and dad, on the right, and friends on the left," said the event manager.

Ria was curious to see what her cake would look like. When Dave opened the box, he saw his daughter stood completely paralyzed after seeing the cake.

"Wow, that cake is amazing!" Ria exclaimed.

The two-layered pink cake with strawberry buttercream had a musical theme. The top layer had the words: Happy Birthday to our Rockstar iced on it, and the side of the second layer was a beautiful sparkling pink mic and guitar. Below it Ria was written in musical notes.

Everyone sang Happy Birthday, and then Ria cut the cake. Dave had ordered a special cake for the boys too. It was a soccer football-shaped cake iced with the boy's favorite team jerseys. The brothers hugged each other when they saw the cake.

The siblings hugged each other. The cakes were delicious, and Dave and Mariah proudly looked on at their children.

About ten minutes before midnight and the start of the New Year, Dave said, "Attention everyone! We have an announcement to make!" Mariah said. The room went silent.

"As well all know, my children turned 16 today, and another pleasant year has passed, but the ending of this year was different. I am with my family this year! And I am pleasantly surprised to see my three young kids have grown up so fast. They can make their own independent choices and with this note, Mariah and I are grateful this year also has passed without any hindrance or violence." Dave said.

"Let us begin the countdown!" Kamran shouted.

The group walked over to the balcony as they heard loud shouts, " 7…6…5...4…3…2…1… Happy New Year!

The group wished each other Happy New Year! Dave popped another bottle of champagne and poured a little in each glass, and once again, everyone toasted.

"Guys, I am going to the washroom! I will be right back!" Ria said as she walked out of the room.

***

Outside the hall, where there was only silence, our hero stood against the wall with darkness in her eyes.

"Even though today, tonight has been so fun, why is my mind and heart continuously indicating that the future isn't all rosy? There are threats, dangers, obstacles, and whatnot! I can sense the screams of innocent lives. There is a heaviness in my chest," thought Ria as she tried to shake those thoughts but failed to do so.

"Enjoy the New Year. I give you this much grace, period. Once you return home, be prepared as I am coming for you," an eerie voice whispered in Ria's ear.

"It's far from over. Playing with monsters, entering the wormhole, that was all a warm-up. You will pay Ria, you have to...," the voice trailed off.

Ria froze in terror.

www.ingramcontent.com/pod-product-compliance
Lightning Source LLC
LaVergne TN
LVHW041020150826
845672LV00001B/148

* 9 7 9 8 8 9 1 8 6 5 8 9 1 *